"Veera Hiranandani's storytelling is exquisite and compelling. For Nisha, like so many of us, home is a complicated place and this heartbreaking and hopeful novel reminds us that even in places where there is great loss and strife, there is deep joy, renewed faith. *The Night Diary* is a treasure for young readers who are searching for their place in the world, who are determined to bring home with them wherever they go."

—Renée Watson, author of Coretta Scott King Award and Newbery Honor–winning *Piecing Me Together*

"Veera Hiranandani is a master storyteller. This riveting and important book speaks to the power of love in a world divided by hate and raises questions that still need to be asked seventy years after its events took place. Nisha and her story are a part of me now. My question is how do we make this a 'community read' for the whole world?"

—James Howe, author of *The Misfits*

"Nisha's sweet, sheltered world disappears overnight when her country splits in two—now Hindus must live in India, Muslims in Pakistan. But Nisha's both. Where can her family be safe? Hiranandani's story is set in an historical time little known to American children, but she tells it in a way that makes it accessible, timely, interesting and real."

—Kimberly Brubaker Bradley, author of Newbery Honor–winning *The War That Saved My Life*

★ "Believable and heartbreaking . . . A gripping, nuanced story of the human cost of conflict appropriate for both children and adults."                                              —*Kirkus Reviews*, starred review

★ "This rich, compelling story, which speaks to the turbulence surrounding India's independence and to the plight of refugees, should be in all libraries."

—*School Library Journal*, starred review

★ "The diary format gives her story striking intimacy and immediacy, serving as a window into a fraught historical moment as Nisha grapples with issues of identity and the search for a home that remain quite timely."

—*Publishers Weekly*, starred review

★ "Nisha and Amil, with their individual interests, talents and convincingly changeable relationship, are protagonists sure to appeal to young readers."    —*Shelf Awareness*, starred review

★ "Remarkably poignant...an important historical tale to tell."

—*School Library Connection*, starred review

"Hiranandani (*The Whole Story of Half a Girl*) does a remarkable job conveying the terrors and absurdities of the conflict in ways young readers can understand.... But it's the family's dramatic journey that will keep readers to the end. The finale—unabashedly weepy, deeply cathartic—is as satisfying as a long, cool drink of water."    —*The New York Times*

"Like the poetic novels *Inside Out & Back Again* by Thanhha Lai and *The Year of Goodbyes* by Debbie Levy, *The Night Diary* personalizes the effect of historic events. With Nisha, readers experience the fear and danger of displacement, take joy in a soothing rain and small bowl of lentils, and try to imagine a new, safe home in a faraway place."    —*The Washington Post*

"In this sensitive and ultimately hopeful story of endurance and love, Ms. Hiranandani handles violence and the threat of it deftly, but, as Nisha reflects: 'My childhood would always have a line drawn through it, the before and the after.'"
—*The Wall Street Journal*

"Hiranandani's portrayal of this bloody period of world history, which is rarely studied in American classrooms, is searing and nuanced."
—*Teen Vogue*

"Hiranandani has flawlessly rendered a world-altering historical event through the eyes of a sensitive and perceptive child."
—*The Horn Book*

"Hiranandani's prose shines in both emotion and simple, rich description . . . A clear, compelling, and deeply felt historical novel."
—*Booklist*

"A beautiful story of hope, family, and identity that's accessible and meaningful for today's middle graders."
—*The Amazon Book Review*

"This searing novel is not so much about what's right or wrong with partition but rather what's right and wrong with people caught in historical crosshairs." —*The San Francisco Chronicle*

A NEWBERY HONOR BOOK

A *NEW YORK TIMES BOOK REVIEW*
NOTABLE CHILDREN'S BOOK OF 2018

A *WASHINGTON POST* BEST CHILDREN'S BOOK OF 2018

AN NPR 2018 GREAT READ

A *KIRKUS REVIEWS* BEST BOOK OF 2018

A *SCHOOL LIBRARY JOURNAL* BEST BOOK OF 2018

AN AMAZON BEST CHILDREN'S BOOK OF 2018

A CHICAGO PUBLIC LIBRARY BEST BOOK OF 2018

A SHELF AWARENESS 2018 BEST CHILDREN'S BOOK OF THE YEAR

# The Night Diary

Veera Hiranandani

PUFFIN BOOKS

Western Himalayas

# Nisha's Journey in 1947

NEW DELHI

Central Himalayas

India

Bay of Bengal

*Line as drawn by Sir Cyril Radcliffe during the 1947 India–Pakistan partition, officially announced on August 17, 1947.

PUFFIN BOOKS
An imprint of Penguin Random House LLC, New York

First published in the United States of America by Dial Books for Young Readers,
an imprint of Penguin Random House LLC, 2018
Published in the United States of America by Kokila,
an imprint of Penguin Random House LLC, 2018
Published by Puffin Books, an imprint of Penguin Random House LLC, 2019

Visit us online at penguinrandomhouse.com

THE LIBRARY OF CONGRESS HAS CATALOGED THE DIAL EDITION AS FOLLOWS:
Names: Hiranandani, Veera, author.  Title: The night diary / Veera Hiranandani.
Description: New York, NY : Dial Books for Young Readers, [2018] |
Summary: Shy twelve-year-old Nisha, forced to flee her home with her Hindu family during the
1947 partition of India, tries to find her voice and make sense of the world falling apart around
her by writing to her deceased Muslim mother in the pages of her diary.
Identifiers: LCCN 2017012579 | ISBN 9780735228511 (hardcover) | ISBN 9780735228535 (ebook)
Subjects: | CYAC: Refugees—Fiction. | Diaries—Fiction. | Family life—India—Fiction. |
Hindus—Fiction. | Muslims—Fiction. | India—History—Partition, 1947—Fiction.
Classification: LCC PZ7.H5977325 Ni 2018 | DDC [Fic]—dc23
LC record available at https://lccn.loc.gov/2017012579

Puffin Books ISBN 9780735228528

Printed in the United States of America

Design by Jennifer Kelly
Text set in Adobe Hebrew

1   3   5   7   9   10   8   6   4   2

*For my dad*

# The
# Night
# Diary

July 14, 1947

Dear Mama,

I know you know what happened today at 6:00 a.m., twelve years ago. How could you not? It was the day we came and you left, but I don't want to be sad today. I want to be happy and tell you everything. I'll start at the beginning. You probably already know what I'm telling you, but maybe you don't. Maybe you haven't been watching.

I like turning twelve so much already. It's the biggest number I've ever been, but it's an easy number—easy to say, easy to count, easy to split in half. I wonder if Amil thinks about you on this day like I do. I wonder if he likes being twelve?

We woke up at a little before seven. Amil and I usually sleep through our birth minutes and then when we wake up, we stand next to the last mark we etched into the wall with a sharp rock. No one else knows it's there. I do it for Amil and he does mine and then we compare how much we've grown since last year. Amil has finally caught up with me. Papa says someday Amil will tower over all of us. That's hard to imagine.

Papa gave me your gold chain with a small ruby stone hanging from it. He started giving me the jewelry when I was seven. Now I have two gold bangles, two gold rings, small emerald-and-gold hoop earrings, and the ruby necklace. Papa said I should save the jewelry for special occasions, but lately there are none, so I wear all the jewelry at once and never take it off. I don't know where he keeps all of it, but each year on my birthday, another piece appears at my bedside in a dark blue velvet box with gold trim. When you open it, the blue satin lining winks back at you. Papa always asks for the box back after I take out the jewelry.

Secretly, I want the box more than the jewelry. I want it to be all mine and never have to give it back. I could find any old thing—a pebble, a leaf, a pistachio shell—and put it in the box. Like magic, these things would get to be special at least for a day. Maybe he'll let me have it when your jewelry runs out.

I want to tell you about this diary I'm writing in. Kazi gave it to me this morning wrapped in brown paper, tied with a piece of dried grass. He never gives me gifts on my birthday. I once read an English story where a little girl got a big pink cake and presents wrapped in shiny paper and bows for her birthday. I thought about the little gifts Kazi gives us all the time—pieces of candy under our pillows or a ripe tomato from the garden, sliced, salted, and sprinkled with chili pepper on a plate. Cake and bows must be nice, but is anything better than a perfect tomato?

The diary is covered in purple and red silk, decorated with small sequins and bits of mirrored glass sewn in. The paper is rough, thick, and the color of butter. It is not lined, which I like. I've never had a diary before. When Kazi gave it to me, he said it was time to start writing things down, and that I was the one to do it. He said someone needs to make a record of the things that will happen because the grown-ups will be too busy. I'm not sure what he thinks is going to happen, but I've decided I'm going to write in it every day if I can. I want to explain things to you as if I'm writing a storybook, like *The Jungle Book* except without all the animals. I want to make it real so you can imagine it. I want to remember what everyone says and does, and I won't know the ending until I get there.

Kazi also gave Amil five charcoal drawing pencils. Five! He also made us rice kheer with our pooris. I'm not sure there is anything better tasting in the world. Amil, who normally eats too fast, makes his pudding last extra long, eating the smallest bites he can. I think he just does it so I have to watch him long after I've finished. Every so often he'll look up and smile. I pretend I don't care. Sometimes he saves his sweets for me, but not rice kheer.

Today we were running late, though, and Amil couldn't spend forever eating his kheer because Dadi took our plates away and told us to get ready. Amil started grumbling about school and how he wished he was a grown-up and could work at the hospital like Papa instead. "The drums sound better at a distance," Dadi said like she always does, and rushed us out the door.

Here's another secret, and don't be mad. Amil and I didn't go to school. We headed all the way out of town to the sugarcane field and tried to walk through it like a maze. We broke off pieces to chew. Later we stopped under a shady tree. Amil found bugs to draw and I read. After, we bought potato pakoras at the roadside cart in town, hoping no one would ask why we weren't in school. The pakoras tasted crisp and extra salty. Amil thinks they're too salty, but I like the sting on my tongue that stays long after I've finished eating.

Amil would rather draw and play all day instead of going to school. He would rather do anything besides school. He draws very well. Did you know that? I don't hate school, but I didn't want Amil to be alone on our birthday. When Papa finds out we didn't go to school, he'll be much angrier at Amil than he will at me. That's how it is with Papa and Amil. It hasn't always been like that. Amil used to be Papa's favorite, I think because Amil was always louder, happier, and funnier than I am. But now because Amil isn't small and cute, Papa is different.

When we were about seven or eight, Amil ran away. That's when it started. Papa came home from a long day at the hospital and during dinner he told Amil to stop smiling so much, that it made him look ridiculous. This only made Amil smile more.

Then Papa said, "Amil, you can't read. You play around too much and draw little pictures. You must be more serious or you will become nothing."

"Maybe I should leave. Then you'll be happy," Amil said. He waited for Papa to say something, but Papa didn't. He just turned back to his food. Amil got up and walked straight out of the house. An hour went by and he didn't come back, so I went out to look for him. I looked everywhere, around the garden, the shed, Kazi's and Mahit's cottages, all the places he might go. I even looked in the pantry and in Papa's closet. Papa acted like nothing was happening, but I told Kazi that I couldn't find Amil anywhere and he told Dadi and Dadi told Papa, so Papa went out with a lantern. I stayed awake in my bed wondering what I would do if Amil never came back. I couldn't imagine being in this house, in this life, without him. I heard Papa return and I waited to hear Amil's voice or his footsteps, but I didn't hear anything and began to cry, holding my doll, Dee, tight. At some point I fell asleep. When I woke at first light, Amil slept soundly in his bed next to mine. I wasn't sure if I had dreamed the whole thing.

"Amil," I said, poking him awake, standing over him. "Where did you go? Does Papa know you're back?"

"Papa knows I'm back," Amil said in a dull voice. "I walked into town, but then I kept going. I didn't want to stop. But Papa found me."

"Is Papa mad?" I asked.

"Papa will always be mad at me. It doesn't matter

it I smile or don't smile. I'm just not what he wanted."

"That's not true," I said, and put my hand on his shoulder. He turned away. He might have been right about Papa, though. Since that night he ran away, Papa always seems angry at Amil for being Amil.

Papa left a book on Amil's bed this morning. Normally on our birthday he only gives me the jewelry and we do puja at our temple and offer the gods handfuls of leaves and sweets for a prosperous year, but Papa did not talk about it this morning. Maybe we will go tomorrow. Papa doesn't like to go to temple. We only go on our birthdays and Diwali because Dadi begs us to go. Sometimes Papa walks her there and waits outside for her. I always look forward to going. I drink in the smoky smell of the lamps burning. I even like the metal taste of the holy water on my tongue. The soft sounds of the prayers being chanted and sung make me feel loved, like you're there, watching. But maybe a Hindu temple is the last place you'd be.

Amil's book is beautiful. It's a thick collection of tales from the Mahabharata with gold lettering on the cover and bright colorful pictures inside. Amil will love the drawings, but he won't read it. Amil says he can't read right because the words jump around and change on him. Papa thinks he's lying so he doesn't have to do his schoolwork. But I know he's not. I see the way he studies the writing, his eyes squinted, his face pinched. I see how hard he tries. He even turns the book upside down sometimes, but he says nothing helps. I think it's because Amil is a little bit magical. His eyes turn everything into art. Maybe Papa thought if he brought him a really good book, Amil would read it.

Papa didn't say anything about skipping school today. I hope our headmasters don't send a messenger with a note. Now I'm tired and must drink my warm milk and go to bed. Amil is already sound asleep, making little whistling sounds through his nose. I've decided that night is the best time to write to you. That way no one will ask me any questions.

Love, Nisha

July 15, 1947

Dear Mama,

I only have time to tell you one thing tonight because my eyelids are heavier than wet sheets. Papa is very mad. I knew he would be when he found out. Amil's headmaster sent over a message. Mine did not. When Papa found out, he made Amil sit in the corner with no breakfast this morning. Amil didn't ask why I wasn't being punished, even though Papa must have known I skipped, too. I guess the difference is that I do well in school and Amil doesn't. I only ate one of my chapatis and wrapped the other in a napkin. Then I stuck it in my schoolbook for Amil when no one was looking.

I think Kazi likes us best. Papa loves us of course because he's our father and Dadi loves us because she's our grandmother. That's what they're supposed to do, but Papa is too busy to do a lot of liking and Dadi is too old. Papa works every day, even on Sunday. I guess he has to since he's a doctor. People leave gifts on our doorstep all the time, like flowers and sweets for the wonderful things he has done for them. Sometimes

I think Papa's not real. He leaves early with the cool morning air and never makes a sound. Sometimes when he comes back late at night and kisses me good night in my sleep, I wake up and see him. It feels like I'm dreaming.

Love, Nisha

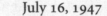

July 16, 1947

Dear Mama,

Kazi has so much energy for us. He always has. When we were younger, maybe five or six, he used to sit cross-legged on the floor and play with us after his work was done. I remember he was the first person to teach Amil how to play cricket in the front of the house, how to throw and bat and catch. Papa never did. I would peer out the window and watch them, laughing hard when Amil missed the ball, since he could hardly see me.

I help Kazi in the kitchen all the time, even though Dadi doesn't want me to. She says I'll marry well and have someone cook for me, just like Kazi does for us. But that doesn't sound like any fun at all. I can't wait to be older and do what Kazi can do. He lets me help him more all the time. I know how to sort the lentils, grind the spices with his marble mortar and pestle, clarify the butter for ghee, and mix the dough for chapatis. I usually finish my schoolwork fast and sneak into the kitchen, when Dadi thinks I'm still working, to help Kazi prepare dinner. He sees me even when he's not looking up. It's like he smells me. He turns and holds up a handful of peas to be shelled. I like to cook things even more than I like to eat them. How does Kazi take all these plain boring foods—bitter vegetables, dried lentils, flour, oil, spices—and turn them into something so warm and delicious every time?

Love, Nisha

July 17, 1947

Dear Mama,

Kazi is right. I was made for writing in a diary. I'd much rather write than talk. I talk very little, mostly just to Amil and Kazi. I feel normal around them. I talk to Dadi and Papa if I have to. But for the rest of the world, the words just don't want to come out, like part of my mouth or my brain is broken. It feels scary to talk, because once the words are out, you can't put them back in. But if you write words and they don't come out the way you want them to, you can erase them and start over. I have the neatest handwriting in my class and get the highest marks on all my compositions. You would be very proud of me.

Amil likes to talk. He likes to run. He likes to laugh. He likes to yell. But he hates writing anything down, except for his drawings. The teachers think he's stupid because he can't read and doesn't do his schoolwork, but they should look at his drawings. Amil draws all sorts of things. Sometimes he draws frightening scorpions and snakes with dark charcoal pencil. He draws every leg, every bump, every little detail. Sometimes he draws me early in the morning when I'm still sleeping. It's strange to look at myself that way, but I like it. It makes me feel like I'm not alone, like someone is always watching over me. Are you, Mama?

Sometimes Amil draws Dadi or Papa when they aren't looking and only shows me. He draws Kazi cooking. He likes to paste lots of paper scraps together with flour and water to make a bigger drawing space. Kazi once gave him a drawing pad. Amil only does his best work on the paper after he practices on his bits of flour bags, ends of newspaper, whatever he can find. He let me touch the drawing pad paper once. It's cloud white, silky smooth. I wonder why Amil is the way he is. I wonder why I am the way I am. I bet you know.

Love, Nisha

July 18, 1947

Dear Mama,

Something very strange happened today. Three men came to our house this afternoon. I don't know why they came. I was doing my homework. Amil tried to do his but mostly doodled. Dadi sat at the table writing letters. Papa was at the hospital. The men knocked on the door. One of them was a teacher at our school who always dyes his gray hair red. His beard is the color of a chili pepper. I didn't recognize the other two men. Dadi looked out the window and called Amil. Then she told us both to go into the kitchen with Kazi, so we did. Her eyes darted back and forth before she answered the door.

All three of us—me, Kazi, and Amil—peeked around the corner. The men spoke so quietly I couldn't hear them. Then they spoke louder. I heard bits and pieces of sentences, words and names I had been hearing Papa talk about to Dadi, seen in the headlines from their newspapers. I turned over the words like puzzle pieces in my head, wondering how they were supposed to fit together: *Pakistan, Jinnah, independence, Nehru, India, British, Lord Mountbatten, Gandhi, partition.*

Dadi nodded and nodded, and the air smelled like the smoke from pipes. She tried to close the door once and one of the men, the tallest one, held the door open, not letting her. I held my breath. Then she finally closed the door and turned around. We came out from our hiding places, but she didn't say a thing. Her eyes were big, and she and Kazi kept giving each other secret looks. Amil asked what happened.

Dadi waved him away, but Amil didn't give up.

"Tell me or I'll scream," he said.

I put my hand over my mouth. I couldn't believe he was being so naughty.

Dadi frowned. "It was nothing to worry about," she said. "And if you scream," she said, wagging her finger angrily at Amil, "your Papa will be the first to know."

Amil's shoulders slumped. Kazi disappeared into the kitchen. I finished my work and helped him clean some green beans and chop the garlic and ginger into the tiniest pieces you ever saw, but Kazi didn't tell me anything and I could tell he didn't want to.

"The men seemed upset," I said later to Amil when we were lying on our beds. "I think something bad is going on."

"I know," said Amil. "I heard them ask when we'd be leaving."

"Why would we leave?" I asked.

"It has something to do with India being free from the British soon," he said.

I wondered what that meant, to be free from the British. Why were they allowed to rule over us in the first place? Didn't they have their own people to worry about? I thought about the men at the door. They seemed calm in that way grown-ups get calm before they get very angry.

"Remember when Papa used to tickle us?" Amil said, turning on his side toward me.

"He hasn't done that in a long time," I replied. When we were little, Papa would tickle us to wake us up. It's so strange to think about that now. I remember trying to like it since Amil liked it so much. Amil would throw his head back and squeal for more. I would grit my teeth and try not to push Papa's hand away. It made me feel like I was falling off a cliff. I asked Amil why he was thinking about that.

"Because I wish he was still that way," Amil said, and turned on his back again.

He closed his eyes and I could hear his breathing slow down. I thought about the old Papa, the one who tickled us. Had Papa changed that much? Or had we just gotten older?

Love, Nisha

July 19, 1947

Dear Mama,

More bad things are happening. When Amil and I walk the mile to our schools, we pass lots of things. First, we walk through the rest of our compound where we live since Papa is the head doctor for the Mirpur Khas City Hospital. The government gave us a large place to live in, much bigger than anyone I know. We have our bungalow, and a coop for the chickens, the flower and vegetable gardens, and the cottages where Kazi and the groundskeeper, Mahit, live. As we walk closer and closer to town, we pass the hospital. Then we pass the jail where all the people have to go when they do things like steal from the markets. Dadi says it's not a jail for the murderers. The murderers go somewhere else. I always try to catch a prisoner's eye when I go to school, since I can see them through the fences. I feel bad for them. Usually they stole because they were hungry. But sometimes there are truly bad ones, too, who just want to be bad, who hurt and steal just for fun. I think I can tell who's bad and who's not. The bad ones smile real big. The good ones don't.

Our schools are right next to each other, the Government School for Boys and the Government School for Girls. Mine is smaller because not all girls go to school, but Papa says it's important to be educated. Today when we walked to school, two older boys started following us. Sometimes this happens. Sometimes they chase Amil, but usually only to scare him. He runs faster than anyone I know, so he always gets away. This time though, the boys started throwing rocks at us. A small one hit the back of my head. Amil pulled my arm and we broke into a run. Amil led us into an alley. We ran through the alley and some gardens, then back onto another dirt road. We found a cluster of mango trees and hid behind them.

"Why did they do that? What did you do?" I whispered at him.

"Nothing! I didn't do anything," he whispered back at me.

I touched the small bump where the rock hit me. We went a different way to school, down another dirt road and through the sugarcane, but it took a long time and we were late. After school we ran all the way home without stopping. When we got home, we stood catching our breath outside the door, so Dadi wouldn't ask why we were out of breath.

"It's because we're Hindus," Amil said. He looked around and started to whisper again. "There are lots of places all over India where the Hindus and Sikhs and Muslims fight one another all the time now. Just not here, yet. Kazi tells me what he reads in the papers. That's why those men came to the house yesterday. They said the Hindus should leave, and they don't want Kazi to live with us."

"Because he's Muslim?" I asked, but Amil didn't answer as he ran into the house and to our room where he worked on his drawings until dinner. I thought about those boys. They were Muslim. Everyone knows who is Muslim, Hindu, or Sikh by the clothes they wear or the names they have. But we all have lived together in this town for so long, I just never thought much about people's religions before. Does it have to do with India becoming independent from the British? I don't see how those two things go together.

Sometimes Amil knows things that I don't. He talks to people more and goes to the market with Kazi. He has lots of friends at school. He doesn't mind if his words come out right, or not. I wish I were more like Amil. I don't have any friends except Sabeen. All the kids play together at my school no matter what religion we are. Sabeen is Muslim, and she and I always have lunch together. She doesn't have many friends because she doesn't stop talking and never listens. I don't mind. I'm a good listener.

Nobody ever mentions the fact that you were Muslim, Mama. It's like everyone forgot. But I don't want to forget. The truest truth is that I don't know any other children whose parents are different religions. It must be a strange thing that nobody wants to talk about. I guess we're Hindu because Papa and

Dadi are. But you're still a part of me, Mama. Where does that part go?

Love, Nisha

July 20, 1947

Dear Mama,

I've been thinking about you a lot lately. I always do around my birthday. Papa told us once that I came out the right way, but Amil came out the wrong way, feetfirst. Amil once asked Dadi if he was the reason you died. Dadi told him to stop thinking such awful things and close his mouth. But I wonder it, too. I hope Amil doesn't think about it too much.

There is one large picture of you that Papa keeps on his bookshelf, with a garland draped over it. Your hair is pulled back into a bun and you have kohl liner on your eyes. You look like a movie star. Amil looks like you with his long nose and wide eyes. I look more like Papa. I have his round face and small mouth, but I wished I looked more like you, Mama.

Sometimes the sadness about you being gone comes and finds me after not being there for a while. Something makes me think about you and then I get sad for a long time. Dadi never kisses me. She only pats my hand. She braids my hair and gives me cardamom milk when I'm sick. But it's not the same. Sabeen's mom walks home with her after school every day. I watch the backs of them as they walk down the road, Sabeen's mother's hips swaying, her hand in Sabeen's, while Sabeen tells her everything about her day. What would your hand feel like holding mine?

I talk to your picture and you watch me with your eyes. When I ask you if you can see us from somewhere, if you think Amil is smart, or if I'll be able to talk in front of other people someday, your eyes say yes to it all.

Love, Nisha

July 21, 1947

Dear Mama,

Kazi tells me stories about you once in a while. I hardly ask him to tell me about you, though, because I'm afraid that the stories might run out. I want to save them, like a treat. This afternoon, I used his mortar and pestle to grind coriander seeds, first crushing them as hard as I could, then twisting the pestle in circles to flatten them and make them into a powder. As soon as they broke under the weight of the pestle, I smelled the warm, soapy scent of them. Kazi chopped onions holding a wooden stick between his teeth so he wouldn't cry.

I asked him if you liked to cook. Kazi shook his head, taking the stick out of his mouth. "She never set foot in the kitchen. She liked to paint. She'd go off to the back of the house and paint and paint. She had to be reminded to eat, she was that sort," he said, and put the stick back in his mouth. Just like Amil, I thought, who always ate the bare minimum in a hurry, hardly tasting it, and then begged to be excused so he could go back to his drawings or watch the older boys in the neighborhood play cricket. I want to be like you, Mama, but I can't understand anyone who forgets about food. Kazi took the stick out again.

"It's your papa who likes to cook. That's where you get it from."

My mouth dropped open. Papa doesn't even make his own tea, I thought.

"Before he hired me, he did the cooking for your mama, and when they had guests, they'd pretend she did the cooking. She'd even dip her fingers in the curry so her nails would be yellowed from the turmeric."

I shook my head. I couldn't imagine any of it, Papa cooking, Papa pretending. Papa and Mama pretending together, here in this house.

"Your papa told me," Kazi said, reading my mind. He moved on to a pile of green chilies, slicing them into tiny slivers.

I still didn't believe him. I'm sure you liked to cook, Mama, even just a little bit.

"Why doesn't he hang up her paintings?" I couldn't say this louder than a whisper. I knew Papa kept her paintings in the corner of his study behind a wooden rocking chair. Sometimes I'd sneak looks at them.

Kazi looked down at his cutting board. "I think he feels sad when he looks at them."

I nodded.

"They were very brave, you know," he told me. "I don't know anyone who did what they did."

I tilted my head and paid close attention. I could tell the way Kazi's voice lowered, he wanted to tell me something important.

"Their families were completely against their marrying. Papa's old school friend, a Hindu priest, agreed to marry them in secret. When they first came here, they were ostracized from the community, even though all kinds of people get along here. But marriage has always been different."

He sliced a few more chilies, and I twisted and pressed the pestle into my coriander powder even though it was fully crushed.

"I needed a cooking job since the restaurant I worked at closed," he said, and paused his chopping again, holding the knife still above the sliced chilies. "I asked at several restaurants and homes, but everyone seemed to have enough help. I was getting desperate, so I decided to knock on the door nobody wanted to knock on. Your papa invited me in and had me cook aloo tikki, your mother's favorite dish. He presented it to your mama. She tasted it and her eyes lit up. I've been here ever since. Your papa is such a good doctor that he quickly earned the respect of his patients in Mirpur Khas, and they began to be accepted in the community. Just as things were getting better, she was gone, your mama. Only three years after they came here." Kazi looked down and cleared his throat.

I took in Kazi's words, let them dance and twirl in my head, replayed them over and over like a beautiful piece of music. I can't stop thinking about it, Papa having secrets with you. Papa cooking before Kazi came. You and Papa marrying against everyone's wishes in secret. What would it have been like if you lived, Mama? These things Kazi tells me are the memories I was supposed to have. They explode in my mind like firecrackers.

Love, Nisha

July 22, 1947

Dear Mama,

Dr. Ahmed came over tonight. He's Papa's friend at the hospital. They are the only doctors there. Papa does more of the checkups and surgeries, and Dr. Ahmed helps women have babies. He comes to our house about once a month. He and Papa smoke their pipes and stay up late playing cards. It's the only time Papa smokes a pipe. Usually I hear them talking loudly, laughing sometimes. Papa also only laughs like that with Dr. Ahmed. But tonight, as I lay in my bed with my mosquito net floating like a ghost around me, I did not hear any laughing. They spoke low. I heard the names again, Gandhi, Jinnah, Nehru, Mountbatten. They talked about bad things in the Punjab, rioting, killing.

Dadi and Papa are having lots of whispering conversations at night, too. They sit in the kitchen and I can't hear their words, but I hear murmurs and spoons clinking around in cups and Dadi's slippers shuffling about as she makes Papa tea.

Here's another secret, Mama. I'm jealous of Papa

because he has his mother and I don't. No mother shuffles about in her slippers making me tea. I wonder if Papa's jealous of me since his papa died a long time ago.

I asked Amil today what he thinks is happening. He says Kazi told him it's true. The British people are going to free India, but there's talk of India being separated into two countries, where Muslims have to go one place and the Hindus, the Sikhs, and every-body else have to go to another place. I told him that sounded insane. Why would India suddenly become two countries?

"I don't know why but it's true," Amil said.

I swallowed hard so no tears would come. "Kazi would never leave us. We're a family. We'll stay to-gether."

"How can you know?"

"Because of Mama. We're part Muslim, too."

"Shush! We're not supposed to talk about that," Amil hissed at me.

I wanted to smile because nobody ever tells me to shush, but I didn't, and it's not true either. No one ever told us not to talk about it. What if I want to talk about it, Mama? What if it's the only thing I want to talk about?

Love, Nisha

July 23, 1947

Dear Mama,

Today I woke up thinking about Kazi and followed the smells of breakfast into the kitchen. I stood by the door and watched him frying pooris. He turned and saw me and motioned me over. I came and he handed me a lump of the soft dough. I squeezed it and squeezed it. I breathed in a big gulp of air, let it out, and asked him if he would have to leave us soon, when everyone goes in different directions. He looked at me and smiled, then bent down and held my face. His hands were greasy and coated in flour. I could see his eyes get big and glassy like he might even cry.

He told me I was like a daughter to him and that I'd always be with him in his heart. Then he told me not to knead the dough too hard or it would fry up like a rock. I didn't say anything else. It took a lot of energy to ask that question. I wished he had answered it. I don't know when I'll be able to ask it again.

Love, Nisha

July 24, 1947

Dear Mama,

I used to think of people by their names and what they looked like, or what they did. Sahil sells pakoras on the corner. Now I look at him and think Sikh. My teacher, Sir Habib, is now my Muslim teacher. My friend Sabeen is happy and talks a lot. Now she's my Muslim friend. Papa's friend, Dr. Ahmed, is now a Muslim doctor. I think of everyone I know and try to remember if they are Hindu or Muslim or Sikh and who has to go and who can stay.

Amil said it's good that we will be free from the British, but what does that mean? Doesn't freedom mean you can choose where you want to be? Maybe Amil was making up things. He does that sometimes. Once in a while he tells me Kazi has a sweet for us when he doesn't or that Papa's home early when he's not. Amil thinks he's being funny.

I want to ask Dadi, but she never tells me anything, at least anything important. She just tells me to go off and get my chores or schoolwork done. I have a plan. I'm going to wake up early and catch Papa in the morning before he leaves for the hospital. If I wait for him at the table before the sun comes up, look right at him, and speak loudly, he'll be so surprised, he'll have to answer me.

Love, Nisha

July 25, 1947

Dear Mama,

Today nothing went right at all, and I'm so glad I have this diary now to tell you about it. I slept too late and Papa was already gone. Amil told me that at his school a Hindu boy called a Muslim boy a very bad word that I can't even write down. They got into a big fight, and now they're both suspended from school for a week. Amil said when they were fighting, all the Hindu boys chanted on one side and the Muslim boys chanted on the other. Everything is different now, even though it's exactly the same. I can see it all around us, but I don't know what to call it. It's like a new sound I can hear in the air.

Amil and I went our secret way again so nobody can chase us. We've done this before. I hate to tell you, Mama, but lots of boys like to pick on Amil because he's very skinny, has hardly any muscles in his arms, isn't that good at cricket, and sits in the corner and draws everyone. There are some boys who like him because he's so funny, but the tougher boys don't. Sometimes Amil will draw those boys looking mean and monster-like and leave the drawings on the ground for people to step on. The boys always come after him, but Amil is too quick for them. He likes to draw the girls, too, and makes them extra beautiful with very long eyelashes. His favorite is Chitra. She's the tallest, prettiest girl I know. After school he'll find her, hand a drawing to her, and run away. She always drops it on the ground, but I see her smile when he gives it to her. She always looks before she lets it go. I think the girls like him better than the boys.

Papa didn't get home until late and went to his room without any dinner. Kazi only made dal and paratha stuffed with potatoes. I lie on my bed and wonder what the air will sound like tomorrow. You know what I wish, Mama, more than anything in the world? That I could spend just one day with you, so I'd know what your skin looks like up close and the sound of your voice. I'd know the scent of you, like I know how Papa always smells like hospital soap, smoke, and the pistachio nuts he carries in his pocket. Then I could think about that when I write these words, and when I try to fall asleep.

Love, Nisha

July 26, 1947

Dear Mama,

Amil says we have to go through our secret path every day. It's too risky to walk on the street now. I told him it was his fault because he drew too many angry pictures of the boys who chase him. He just laughed. Amil laughs when he doesn't know what to say. I hate cutting through the sugarcane. My legs and arms get all scratched up. When I walk I like to think of dinner and what Kazi might be making. It distracts me. Sometimes I think of new things to make. I wonder how pistachios crushed with rosewater syrup and sweet cheese would taste. I think of a stew made with lamb, tomatoes, cream, and apricots. I think of how garlic and gingerroot smell sizzling in ghee or the way dry rice feels falling through my fingers.

I said to Amil if we told all the kids at our schools the truth about Mama, maybe we could be friends with everyone. Maybe it would be a good thing now, instead of a bad thing. Maybe we could stay and not have to leave.

"Nisha, that's the stupidest thing you've ever said. Maybe you should always keep your mouth shut," Amil told me.

I know you may not want to hear this, Mama, but I spit on his toes and ran back out to the road and walked by myself all the way home. I held my breath because I was so afraid. But no one chased me, even though I saw some of the boys that don't like Amil on the other side of the road. Then I realized the only reason they chase us is because of Amil and his ridiculous drawings and his big mouth. The boys aren't mad at me. I'm safer by myself.

Love, Nisha

July 28, 1947

Dear Mama,

I'm very sorry, but I couldn't write to you yesterday and tell you the rest of the story. I needed all the feelings to stop boiling like a pot of dal and be cool enough for me to taste them.

After I left Amil, I came home first and went into the kitchen. I sat on a stool and watched Kazi chop vegetables and grind spices. He asked if I wanted to slice the okra, but I hate okra. I truly don't know why anyone likes it. When it cooks, it smells like wet dirt. I shook my head no. He asked me if I wanted to grind peppercorns. I shook my head no again. Kazi just shrugged and handed me a chapati to eat. I chewed and stayed silent just like Amil said I should. Maybe he's right. Maybe it's easier that way. An hour went by but Amil didn't come home. Those boys could have found him, beaten him, and left him lying on the ground. My breathing got faster. What if he was hurt, alone, and bleeding? What if it was my fault?

I started to sweat. I opened my mouth, closed it, then opened it again, and the words came out slowly.

I told Kazi about the boys, Amil's drawings, our secret path, and how we went different ways today. I didn't tell him what Amil said.

Kazi put down the mortar and pestle and took off his apron.

"It's good you told me, Nishi," he said. Then he took my hand, squeezed it hard, and asked me to show him the path.

We told Dadi we were going to the market, which was probably not a good idea since I never go to the market with Kazi. But before she could respond, we left. We walked on the dirt path and through the sugarcane all the way to school, but no Amil.

Kazi said we had to tell Papa. I shook my head hard and bit my lip to stop the tears. But it didn't stop them and they fell on my nose, my chin, the ground. Kazi pulled me toward the hospital.

We stepped into the building. I never like going there. First there's the smell. It smells clean and dirty all at once—rubbing alcohol, flowers, vomit, and pee. Everything is white or brown. The outside is brown brick, and the inside has light brown cement floors, white walls, and white sheets on the beds. I hate to see sick people, old men and women lying in beds moaning, grabbing on to the nurses' sleeves. Or worse, I'll see a girl my age, too thin, yellow skin, blank eyes, leaning against her mother waiting to be seen, and I'll wonder why she is there and I'm here, able to run, smile, and eat. People die there all the time. Amil likes it at the hospital. He runs around and gives all the old lady patients flowers. He's not afraid of the sick the way I am.

One of the nurses came up to us. Kazi asked for Papa. We stood and waited in the hallway until Papa came. He stood with crossed arms and looked at me before he spoke.

"What brings you here, Nisha?" he finally asked.

"It's Amil," I whispered. There was a nurse standing near us, folding sheets.

"I can't hear you, Nisha," he said, his eyebrows scrunched together the way they do before he gets really angry.

"He's lost," I told him as loud as I could and stared at my feet.

"I see," he said. "That's not what he told me. Amil!"

I jumped as Papa called out Amil's name. Then Amil hobbled slowly out of one of the hospital rooms on crutches. He had a bandage on his leg. I ran up to him and hugged him. He didn't hug me back.

"Did they beat you?" I whispered in his ear.

"Did who beat you?" Papa said.

Amil and I looked at each other. I wondered what he had told Papa.

"No one!" Amil yelled, and began to cry.

"Who?" demanded Papa.

"Some Muslim boys," Amil answered through his sobbing.

"Stop crying," Papa said with disgust. He hates it when we cry. For as long as I remember, crying makes Papa get either angry or just walk away.

I looked toward Kazi, but he wasn't there anymore. Had he left? I blinked to make sure I was right.

"They didn't beat me; I ran away," Amil said, and rubbed his eyes furiously with the backs of his hands. He took a deep breath and straightened his shoulders. "I was faster than them. I'm always faster than them."

"So they've come after you before," Papa said.

Amil nodded.

"Nisha," Papa said, "is this true?"

"Yes, Papa," I said.

"Are you doing anything to provoke them?" Papa asked.

Amil's face reddened. "No, Papa."

It wasn't exactly true, but I didn't dare tell Papa that. This time it was different. The chasing, the rocks. Before it was just stupid things boys do. Now, it all had a mysterious anger to it. I don't know what's happening, Mama. I wish you could explain it to me. I'm becoming more and more afraid to ask anyone else all the things I really want to know.

Love, Nisha

July 29, 1947

Dear Mama,

Last night a few hours after I fell asleep Amil woke me up. He lifted up my mosquito net and crawled into my bed next to me. His body felt hotter than mine, but dry as silk, not sweaty like me.

"Want to know what it felt like?" he asked. A low, full moon glittered in the sky, and the light spilled through our window like a silver sun. He held his big, swollen scorpion bitten foot up in the air. I nodded, trying to shake the sleep away.

"I ran through an alley to get away from the boys, and my foot slipped out of my sandal. I saw the scorpion on my ankle. I tried to shake it off and then it stung me. It felt like an electric shock throughout my whole body. I thought I was going to die, but for some reason I wasn't scared."

"Did it hurt?" I asked him.

"Only after, when it started to swell." He lowered his foot down carefully.

I turned to face him. "I'm sorry I left you. Do you think those boys would really beat you?"

Amil shrugged. "I'll just keep running. Hopefully Papa will let me stay home until my foot gets better."

I nodded and made a silent promise to myself that I would somehow convince Papa to let Amil stay home until he could run.

"Don't ever leave me like that," I said, turning away from him toward the wall.

"Where would I go?" he said, and we both fell asleep under my mosquito net. We used to sleep like that all the time, but when we turned eight, Papa said we had to sleep in our own beds. When we have bad dreams or I guess if someone's foot is swollen because of a scorpion bite, then we don't listen to Papa. We quickly move to our own beds in the morning, so no one ever knows. Sometimes I wonder if we would have different rules if you were around, Mama.

Love, Nisha

July 30, 1947

Dear Mama,

When we came out for breakfast this morning Papa sat at the table. I can't remember the last time Papa had breakfast with us on a weekday. We ate our chapatis and dal quietly. I took a sip of my milk. Papa took a sip of his tea. Then Dadi sipped, and then Amil, really loud. We were making strange music. I had to hold back a smile.

After we were finished, Kazi took away the plates and went back into the kitchen. Papa cleared his throat, a big rumbling sound. This is what he said: "You won't be going to school for a little while. Things are not safe. Dadi and I will give you your lessons."

I couldn't believe my ears! Dadi never reads anything but a newspaper once in a while and Papa's never home. How could they possibly give us our lessons? But that's what Papa said. When Amil heard, he jumped up and laughed and then gave out a yelp because he stepped on his swollen foot. He sat down quickly, and I thought I saw a little smile sneak out from the corner of Papa's lips. Then Papa rubbed his hands together the way he always does before he gets up and pushes his chair away. I wasn't going to let Papa walk away without explaining more. Was this only because of the boys chasing Amil?

I took a very deep breath and spoke loud and clear so Papa would not ask me to repeat it.

"Why?"

"Why what?" Papa said, already starting to get up.

My words were stuck. I pressed my lips together. My heartbeat started to race. I took another breath. He now stood tall, looking at me, waiting. I had to keep going. I wanted to know more than I wanted to be silent. "Why isn't it safe? Is it because the British are leaving?" I asked, and felt my body relax a little now that the words were out.

Papa sat back down. He rubbed his chin for a second and then he spoke. "Soon, India will be independent from British rule, which is a good thing. They have ruled over us for almost two hundred years, treating us like second-class citizens in our own country. But it looks like this country is going to be split in half like a log, partitioned down the middle," he said, drawing a line through the air. "Mirpur Khas won't be in India anymore. This land will be in a new country called Pakistan."

Amil and I looked at each other. Amil said the word Pakistan out loud.

Papa went on. "Jinnah, the leader of the Muslim League, wants a place for Muslims to be fairly represented. Nehru, the leader of the Indian National Congress wants to be the first Prime Minister of

India. Gandhi wants everyone to stay together, which is what I want, but most people aren't like Gandhiji. When you divide people, they take sides. There's a lot of confusion and fear out there. I don't want you to get hurt."

I nodded, but I couldn't take in all that Papa was saying. Were we just at the mercy of leaders who couldn't agree? Who would people listen to? I thought about Gandhi. I had seen lots of pictures of him in the newspaper, the thin man who wore nothing but a dhoti and glasses. Papa said he was a great man who believed India was a place where people of all religions could live together in peace. When people made him unhappy with their stupid fighting, instead of yelling at them or fighting with them, he wouldn't eat until people were peaceful again. And Papa told us a lot of people listened to him. But I guess not everyone.

When we were nine, Papa took us on an overnight train ride to Bombay to see Gandhi. I remember how Amil hated that train ride. Dadi and I tried to keep him busy with songs and card games and snacks so he wouldn't keep jumping up or trying to talk to everyone. Papa just read his papers and books. But when we got there after many hours, the crowds stood so thick, thousands of people from many villages, that I only got a small glimpse of him, far away in his white dhoti, waving. Now I wonder if I had only imagined it. Could Gandhi fix things? Would we really have to leave? Amil opened his mouth to say something, but Papa put his hand up.

"That should answer your questions," he said. Then he rubbed his hands together one more time, got up, and set out for the hospital. Dadi told us to stay at the table, and we did some simple addition problems on the abacus until Dadi started making her funny teeth-sucking noises and waved us away. The thought of not going to school made my body heavy with sadness. I'm going to miss school. I like being around different people even if I don't want to talk to them. I like having tasks set before me so I can busy myself without thinking too much. I don't like thinking about things I can't understand.

Love, Nisha

July 31, 1947

Dear Mama,

Kazi has been behaving differently. He let me sort the lentils yesterday and soak some beans, but when I asked him if I could grind the peppercorns he told me it would make me sneeze like last time and that I should spend more time with my books since I wasn't in school.

The day went so slowly without school. It felt like a Sunday which is normally a treat, but now it's too much and we are sick with our freedom. Amil and I went outside after Dadi made us write the alphabet ten times even though I've been writing my alphabet since I was six. This is not so easy for Amil, though. He says letters to him are like bugs and grass waving in the wind. They are not flat. They move and change in his mind. He says he writes what he sees in the moment. I look at his paper. He doesn't do a list, he just puts each letter in its own place on the paper, sometimes it's the right way, sometimes it's upside down, sometimes it's only part of the letter, and sometimes it's facing the opposite direction. He decorates them with swirling snakes and hungry scorpions. It's the most beautiful thing I've ever seen, but Dadi comes over and sucks on her teeth.

I bet, Mama, that's why you liked to paint. Because you could see things that no one else could, just like Amil. I wish I were like that. I see exactly what's in front of me. Sometimes it's so clear, it hurts my eyes.

Love, Nisha

August 1, 1947

Dear Mama,

This is what I did today: I got up, had a chapati and a bowl of yogurt, and sat at the table helping Dadi fold the linen napkins. Then she made me do my alphabet. I told her I can write the alphabet backward a hundred times in my sleep. She slapped my hand and told me to run and play with Amil, who was nowhere to be found. But I didn't care. I just didn't want to sit at the table with Dadi anymore.

I spotted Amil sitting in the garden among the cucumbers. He was counting them. We have twenty-seven new ones, he told me. We each picked a cucumber and ate it. It was crunchy and slightly warm and sweet from the sun. Now we have twenty-five.

As we ate, I could hear Amil chewing. I hate listening to people chew, especially crunchy things. I hate hearing their tongues smacking around. Swallowing is the worst part. It makes me think of the chewed-up food going down their throats slow and wet, and I want to scream. I chewed louder so I couldn't hear him anymore. Then we went inside because it was so hot and took a nap. Dadi woke us a little later and told us to sweep. Amil said no and ran out the door before Dadi could even call him. He'll probably hide in the garden shed etching pictures on the soft wooden walls with sharp rocks. He once said if we ever moved, he would leave our story on the walls. I always thought we'd never leave, but now who knows? I thought of a stranger, a boy or a girl, finding Amil's pictures and wondering what they meant.

Sometimes I go look and see what he's added. There's Papa with his stethoscope and Kazi stirring a pot of something. There's Dadi sewing. There's me and Amil sitting in a garden. They are simple, rough pictures. There is one where Amil is looking up at me, and I look much bigger than he does. I wonder if Amil really feels so much smaller. If I could draw, I would draw Amil like a long branch, tall and thin, but breakable. I would be small and curled up, hiding somewhere in the shade.

I didn't mind sweeping. I like the soothing *brush brush* sound. After sweeping I went into the kitchen, sat on the stool, and watched Kazi stir and chop. I sniffed the air. Coriander. Garlic. Spinach. The tangy scent of chickpeas soaking in a bowl. I felt hungry and grabbed a few radishes I saw sitting by the windowsill, cut them up, sprinkled them with cayenne pepper and lemon juice, and popped each piece in my mouth enjoying the sour heat.

I stood after I finished my snack. Kazi pushed a pot of lentils to be sorted toward me, his head still down.

"Are you mad at me, Kazi?" I whispered. I've found that whispering gets people's attention even better than being loud.

He looked up and stared for a moment. Then his face turned soft.

"No, no. I could never be mad at someone as sweet as you. I'm just mad at the world," he told me.

I wanted to ask him why, but then I thought of how the answer might make my stomach hurt. So I kept quiet and went through the lentils, making sure there were no little pebbles or grit and rinsed them off with water. I slipped a shiny one in my mouth and tried to chew it, but it almost broke my teeth.

We had my favorite spinach dish for dinner, sai bhaji with poori, and I ate up every last bit. I think Kazi made it just for me. He even made gulab jamun for dessert, as if it were a party.

I remember when we used to have parties. Papa would have his brothers over with my aunties and cousins. Some of our neighbors would come, and Papa would smoke cigars or his pipe with the other men outside on the veranda. The women would sit in the main room, drink tea, and pass around samosa and kebab. Then we'd all have a huge feast with mutton biryani, dal, curries, poori, paratha, and pakora. We hardly ever ate meat except for parties. My mouth watered at its richness.

Afterward, Papa would turn on his record player, and all the kids would have a cricket game outside until we came in exhausted and lay our heads on the floor. Someone would pop a sweet in my mouth and send me off to bed. There was so much noise and laughter that late at night I'd start talking to my cousins without even thinking. My voice would slip into all the other voices. It was the me I was underneath, the me that usually stays inside.

Ever since Amil and I have gotten a little older, Papa doesn't like to have parties. I'm not sure why. Papa used to be happier. Or maybe Amil and I used to be happier. I'm not sure which.

Tonight I pretended we were having a party as we ate our gulab jamun. I like to make mine last as long as possible, the rosewater syrup tickling my tongue. Then I asked Amil to play chess with me before we went to bed.

When Papa came in to kiss us good night, I could smell the rosewater on his lips from dessert. It's his favorite, too. I rolled over and whispered in his ear, "When can we go back to school, Papa?" Amil sat up on his bed and looked at Papa. But Papa just patted my head and left. I don't ask many questions, so it would be fairer if he answered the few I ask. He should be more appreciative. I could be like Amil and ask a question every five seconds, but he doesn't answer many of those either.

Love, Nisha

---

August 2, 1947

Dear Mama,

Today Amil and I were playing chess when we heard people yelling outside. It was so far away we ignored it at first. It's strange how good Amil is at chess since he can barely write a sentence. This is one way I know Amil is so smart. He wins every game, but I still like trying. Someday I'll win. I've come close. I know Amil feels bad for always winning. He always says "Checkmate, sorry." I tell him it's okay. I like that he's good at chess and drawing, since I always do much better at school. Papa taught Amil how to play when he was six, and then Amil taught me when Papa didn't have time to play with him anymore. I think it's that Amil started beating Papa and Papa didn't like it.

As we played, the yelling grew louder. I still couldn't hear what they were saying. We ran to the window and saw men walking up the hill holding torches. Dadi, who was sewing, got up and grabbed us away from the window, brought us into the kitchen, and pushed us into the pantry. I stood near the large tins of rice and could smell the cinnamon sticks which sat on a shelf right near my face. Kazi had already gone to his cottage for the day. Dadi hissed at us to stay still. Then she ran out and turned off the lanterns in the main room. She came back into the pantry with us breathing hard and pulled us in the corner with her. She threw an old tablecloth over us and began to pray. We crouched down as she rocked back and forth and whispered her prayers to Lord Brahma, Vishnu, and Shiva.

Someone banged on our front door. I reached for Amil's hand in the darkness and he held it tight. His hand was cold and wet like a fish. The door banged again and then we heard it burst open and people walking around in our house. We heard things being knocked down, a bowl, a lantern, the table. Amil's hand felt even colder but I held on.

After a while the sounds quieted down. We waited many minutes after the silence. Then we heard Kazi's voice calling for us. I let out the breath I felt like I had been holding the entire time. We unfolded ourselves from the corner of the pantry and came out. Kazi's eyes were wild and blood trickled down his face like a spider. I felt a rush of nausea and steadied myself by clutching the wall. Dadi moved very quickly and got a clean towel from the kitchen, wrapping Kazi's head tightly while he sat. I had never seen her move so fast. She must love Kazi as much as I do.

Amil and I lit some candles and a lantern that wasn't broken. We picked up the knocked down chairs and table, cleaned the glass from the broken lanterns, and put the books back on the shelf. I found Kazi's favorite big clay bowl he always used for chopped vegetables or mixing dough. It lay smashed to pieces on the kitchen floor. I kneeled by his chair and showed him a big chunk of it, my hands shaking.

"It's okay, Nishi," he said, and patted my arm. "We'll get another." I nodded and turned so he wouldn't see my tears as I swept up all the pieces. I slipped a small piece in my pocket.

After we cleaned, we sat together at the table, but hardly talked. Nobody went to bed. Dadi kept checking Kazi's head, but he had stopped bleeding. Finally, Papa came home. He stared at us all sitting at the kitchen table, blinking as if he were seeing a vision. Before he could say anything, Dadi told him what happened.

He nodded, his face serious, his eyes glassy and tired looking. He walked over and examined Kazi's head.

"You need stitches," he said calmly. "Amil, go fetch my medicine bag."

When Amil brought it, Papa started cleaning out Kazi's wound with rubbing alcohol. Kazi made a face and sucked in his breath. Amil and I watched with open mouths as he injected Kazi with something that would numb his skin and then started to thread his needle with thick black thread. As the needle pricked Kazi's skin, my stomach flipped. I couldn't watch anymore, but Amil walked closer and Papa started to explain what he was doing. Amil's chest puffed up and he nodded proudly, listening to every word.

Amil loved watching Papa do all his doctor stuff, but I hated blood and needles. I rubbed my forehead, which throbbed in the same place Kazi's gash was.

"Nisha and Amil, it's time to go to sleep," Papa said after he finished and sat down in his big chair. "I need to discuss things with Dadi." Dadi came over and sat in her chair.

"But what happened?" Amil cried, running his hands through his hair. "Who hurt Kazi? What if they saw us? Would we all be dead? Were they after you, Papa?"

Papa squinted at Amil. "After me? What did I do? Everyone has gone crazy. That's all. This was supposed to be a beautiful moment in history. India will soon be a free country, but instead what are we doing? What are we doing?" Papa shook his head and he became quiet. Then he rubbed his eyes. Dadi came over and put her hand on his shoulder.

"Sometimes the world as you know it just decides to become something else. This is our destiny now," he said, still rubbing his eyes.

Dadi spoke to us louder than she usually did, staying by Papa's side. "But you must not worry. We will always keep you safe."

Amil and I nodded. What would have happened if the men found us in the pantry? I had never wondered about being safe before. I just thought I was.

"Yes, yes, of course," Papa said, looking up, his face relaxing. "We'll figure something out." Then he shooed us off.

Amil and I sat cross-legged on his bed facing each other, too frightened to go to sleep. The fear I felt almost seemed like something exciting, and yet I knew it wasn't.

"Our destiny?" I asked Amil. "What is Papa talking about?"

"I guess he means that everybody starts fighting eventually."

"Sometimes you and I fight, but then we make up," I said to him hopefully.

"That's because we're family. We're all we have."

I picked at a loose thread on his bedspread.

He continued. "Do you think it was Muslims or Hindus that came?"

"I don't know," I said.

"If it was Muslims, why would they want to hurt Kazi? What side are we even on?"

"Do we have to take a side?" I asked.

"I think it's safer. That way you know who your enemy is," Amil said, and crossed his arms tightly over his chest.

"But if we don't take a side, then we don't have any enemies."

"I don't think it works that way," Amil said.

"Gandhiji would agree with me," I told him. "And anyway I thought the two sides were supposed to be us and the British. Why are we fighting each other?"

Amil cocked his head to the side, thinking. I wanted to know who the men were, too, but even if I knew the answer, it still wouldn't make any sense.

Me, Amil, Papa, Dadi, and Kazi. That's it. That's the only side I know how to be on. The world seems so tiny now. I don't even really have you, Mama. I try to make you real by writing these letters, but who knows if you're even listening. I wish you could give me a sign.

Love, Nisha

August 3, 1947

Dear Mama,

Today I woke up and found Kazi in the kitchen kneading dough. He gave me some and I sank my fingers into it. I noticed he still had his bandage on. I rolled the dough into a ball and flattened it again into a thin circle. Kazi hummed a song to himself.

"Kazi," I whispered in my strongest whisper. "Why is this happening? I'm twelve now and ready to know everything."

He looked at me and his whole face changed, his mouth smiling wide. I could see almost all his yellow teeth. "And I am four times as much, but I feel like I don't know anything."

I placed my dough on the counter and punched and pounded and punched until I couldn't hear my thoughts. Kazi caught my hands and squeezed. "Stop, Nisha. You will hurt yourself."

I ran out of the kitchen to my room and curled up in the corner, hugging my knees close. I wanted Kazi to come. I waited and waited. If he came it would mean he loved me. He didn't come and I cried until breakfast.

When I came to the table for breakfast, Kazi was not there. Papa was there and Amil was there and Dadi was there. Papa kept his eyes on his food which meant that nobody should talk. We ate in silence, then I brought my plate to the kitchen. Later when Amil and I went outside, we saw Kazi in the garden picking vegetables. I grabbed Amil and pulled him around the back of the bungalow. I asked him why Kazi wouldn't tell me anything.

"I just wish I knew who beat Kazi and why," I said.

"I heard some Muslim homes were burned not that far from here. Maybe they were angry," Amil said, bending over, ripping up pieces of grass.

"So will everyone burn everyone?" I asked.

"I don't know," Amil said, throwing up his hands, letting go of the grass. We watched it float to the ground.

A surge of anger I have never felt before bloomed in my chest. Let all the crazy men come and burn it all down. Let them burn our gardens and the hospital and your picture, Mama, like it was never there at all. We would go somewhere fresh and new where people were happy. All kinds of people practicing all kinds of religions. A place where Papa wasn't gone all the time, where Dadi would know more, and not make strange noises with her teeth, a place where I could go to school safely and make wonderful things in the kitchen with Kazi whenever I wanted. A place where you were alive and would walk to school with me, holding my hand, and nobody would mind that you were Muslim and Papa was Hindu and Amil and I could hold both sides of our parents in our hearts. We could go to a place where Amil didn't see his words differently and I knew how to talk easily in front of people and had real friends. While everything burned to flat black ash, we wouldn't be sad because we'd be in this new place.

Love, Nisha

August 4, 1947

Dear Mama,

It's the middle of the night and I can't go back to sleep. I had a dream that you were alive. You came into my room and lay down next to me on my bed. You looked so real. Your hair was long and loose and you wore an emerald and gold salwar kameez. I touched you and you smiled. You told me you'd take me to your favorite star, that we could actually go there and look down and watch the rest of the world. You carried me up to the sky and we flew toward a bright light. But I couldn't see anything and then you were gone. I was swimming in light all by myself. That's when I woke up sweating and confused. This is your way of visiting me, right, Mama? I feel so happy because now I know you're listening.

Love, Nisha

August 5, 1947

Dear Mama,

Today was the strangest day. Kazi took everything
out of the pantry, the containers of lentils, dried peas,
rice, flour, and spices. He took out all the utensils and
pans and bowls. He wiped down the counters with
rags dipped in water and vinegar. Then he lined things
up, ready to be carried away at any moment. Does this
mean we were leaving? The thought made me dizzy.

Then Papa came home early and sat with us and
took turns playing chess, and he didn't even seem mad
that Amil won. After that, he read from the Mahabharata storybook for a long time. His voice sounded
different, higher, sadder. He read slowly and didn't
stop when he was supposed to at the periods.

"Why did Papa do that?" Amil asked when Papa
left. I lay on my bed, turning my gaze toward the
long wavy crack on the ceiling. I held up my finger
and traced it in the air. Papa had never read us a story
before, not once. In fact, other than my schoolteach-
ers reading out of our textbooks, no one had ever read
to me before. Dadi would sing to us when we were

little and tell us stories that she remembered from her childhood, but she never read out of a book. Did Papa read to me when I was little and I just don't remember?

"He's lonely," Amil said. Maybe he was lonely. Maybe he was scared, too. I've felt lonely many times before. But I didn't think grown-ups could get lonely. Papa's in the hospital all day with people. But when Amil said it, I realized it was the perfect word for Papa. I could see it in his blank eyes every day, his slumped shoulders. I felt sad for him. He must miss you, Mama, in a different way than I do. He misses the time he had with you. I miss the time I didn't have. He must remember the way the house smelled when you were in it, the sound of your voice filling the air, the sight of you painting your pictures. The moment Amil and I were here with our crying, our bottles of milk, our little fingers and toes, you were gone.

"Maybe he'll do it again," I said.

"Maybe," Amil answered.

"He needs to practice. He's a terrible reader," I said.

"Yes, he is terrible, isn't he?" he said, his eyes becoming bright and excited. We both giggled with our hands over our mouths. For some reason it made us happy to think about how terrible he was. I wondered if Papa had trouble seeing letters the right way like Amil. But that couldn't be. He was a doctor. He read all those medical books. I hope he'll read to us again.

Love, Nisha

---

August 6, 1947

Dear Mama,

I have so much to tell you! I'm bursting with it all, and I'm afraid I'll never be able to sleep. Today I wished I could be a singer. Kazi took us to the market and told us to stay close. I hardly ever go to the market. Amil goes with Kazi, and I have always wondered why women and girls don't go to the market more. It's so bright and busy and exciting. Today Kazi didn't want to leave us alone, so we all went, even Dadi. We stayed close to him as he went around and bought some yellow squash, a bag of potatoes, a bunch of peas, since we didn't have any more in our garden, a pouch of cumin seeds, garlic, gingerroot, turmeric root, and two sticks of white rock candy for me and Amil. I knew from the potatoes and peas, that Kazi was going to make samosas, which he hardly ever does. I listened to all the sounds of the market, vendors calling out prices, children laughing and crying, the rush of dried spices, beans, and rice being poured into bags. Then we happened upon a group of boys playing music. They didn't look much older than I was, but I hadn't seen them before. One boy played the sitar, one played a tabla. Another played a bansuri. The boy playing the tabla also sang.

He was a slight boy, with very thick eyebrows and deep-set dark eyes. He had a clear, high-pitched voice, like cold running water. I wondered if they always sang at the market or was it unusual? People gathered around them to watch. The music rippled out in waves over the growing crowd. I could smell cashews roasting and ripe star fruit and the scent seemed to dance with the notes in the air. How lovely would it feel to sing like that, to change the air with my voice, to fill people's ears with such pleasure. The sound cleared its own space and made it seem like everything was okay again. I wondered if it was. I watched them for a long time, not wanting the feeling to leave me. When Kazi was ready to go, Amil and Dadi had to pull me away.

At home I followed Kazi into the kitchen and tugged on his shirt so he'd turn around and look at me. I didn't feel like talking at all today. Watching the boys made me want to be quiet, so I could think about them. I was afraid each word I might utter would somehow fade the memory. Kazi handed me a bowl. He told me how much flour to pour and I mixed the dough. He showed me how to roll it out into circles, cut them in half, and put a spoonful of pea and potato filling in the middle of each one. Then he taught me how to fold the dough over the filling and dab the edges with water before pressing the corners together. Each samosa felt like a small animal, soft and warm in my hand. We worked quietly, me filling the dough, Kazi frying them until they became golden brown.

"Papa's having a party tomorrow," he told me. "Make sure you have your nice clothes ready." His eyes lit up. Sweat and specs of splattered oil dotted his face.

I thought Kazi might be joking. A party? I thought we were supposed to be scared and sad now. How could we have a party? I had to tell Amil. I found him sitting in the garden putting little green beetles in holes he dug, burying them alive.

"That's mean," I said.

"They can crawl back out. I like to watch. They work so hard."

"Well, if they don't they'll die!" I cried.

"But they don't let themselves die," Amil said. "They fight."

"We're having a party," I finally said after watching a beetle work its way back out of a hole.

Amil jumped up and kept jumping while he talked, which he often did. He said he had known it because this morning he saw Papa take out the jasmine incense. Papa says you always burned some before a party.

I asked Amil what he thought the reason was, but he didn't know. We ran back to the kitchen to ask Kazi. Kazi told us Papa would tell us when he got home. Amil and I sat around by the door like lonely dogs and waited for Papa. I read and Amil sketched little beetles crawling out of their holes, and then we heard Papa's heavy step on the stone walk.

"Papa, Papa," we called, running toward him. "Why are we having a party?"

He looked at us and smiled. Then he smoothed my hair. I felt goose bumps pop up all over my arms. Papa never touches me except for an occasional kiss on the forehead at night before bed.

"I want to see our friends and family. It's been too long," he said. Then he sat down on a kitchen chair. He motioned for us to come and sit with him. Dadi left to make tea. He smiled. We smiled back. He asked how school was. We told him we don't go to school anymore because he told us not to.

"Of course. How ridiculous of me," he said. Then his face turned very sad.

"We're leaving soon," is what he said when he had his tea. I wasn't surprised. I had seen the signs. My bottom lip quivered as the news sunk in. He took another sip and we waited.

"Many are going. Some are staying no matter what. But I have you two," he said, looking at each of us. "The other day made me realize we aren't safe. It's only going to get worse."

"Why are people fighting, Papa?" Amil asked. Papa sat back in his chair and began to tell us things he never told us before. I'll try to remember everything he said.

"Everybody thinks they are protecting and defending their people. But we are all people, right? I've never talked about this before, but there were many who were unhappy that I married your mother," he started saying, his eyes wide and alert.

I swallowed. I tried not to move or blink. I was afraid anything might stop Papa from talking about you. He cleared his throat and looked far away at nothing. I blinked because I couldn't help it. Then there was silence. I thought I ruined it with my blink, but he continued. Amil stayed still, too.

"Our families thought we shouldn't be married because your mother was Muslim and I am Hindu. That's why we decided to move here, far away from our families. Let them fight it out themselves. Even though we had many Muslim friends and neighbors, it never matters when it comes to marriage. Many people feel like this, but I don't. If someone comes into the hospital, I treat them no matter who they are or what religion they are. When I open a body up, I see the blood, the muscles, the bones, all the same in every person, like Gandhiji says. Jinnah and Nehru, they are secular men, yet we need two countries instead of one because of religion. They are leading us toward this—this slicing, this partitioning of India," Papa said, chopping his finger through the air.

Then he continued. "My family didn't understand how I could turn away from all the Hindu girls they found for me. I did well in school. I was going to be a doctor. Many families sought out my parents for a match, but my parents wanted me to like the girl. I met your mother because I played on a cricket team, and she and her friends started to watch us on the way back from school. She was younger than I was, only eighteen. I was already in medical college and my classes ended earlier. One day I thought she was smiling at me. When I looked, she wasn't. But then I snuck a look out of the corner of my eye and I could see that smile.

"Once as she was leaving the cricket game, she tripped, spilling her books. I couldn't stop myself. I left the game to help her. She said she hurt her ankle, so I helped her carry her things home. Her friends walked with me, not allowing her to be alone with a strange man. But her family thanked me. They seemed friendly. Then she began stopping by the cricket game every week, and I started walking her and her friends home. Her friends let us walk ahead and talk. We did that for two years. All my friends and family were very angry with me. But I couldn't stop. She was different from any girl I had known. Yes, she was very beautiful, especially when she smiled. She was kind. She made me laugh. But she also understood things about people. She knew how complicated they were."

Amil and I sat there, mouths parted. Papa coughed a little and turned away from us, gazing out the window, but he kept speaking.

"So we married and moved out of our village. Soon after we were married, your Mama's parents died and my father died all in the same year. And then three years later she . . . ," he paused for a few seconds before going on. "Dadi came to live with us after that. My brothers eventually moved closer to us, too."

I let this sink in. How did I not know that your parents, my other grandparents, had died? I had just thought they lived very far away.

"Did Mama have any brothers or sisters?" Amil asked.

Papa was quiet. "A brother and a sister."

I took this in. The uncle and aunt I never met. I think I had heard it before, but I felt like I had imagined it. There are parts of you out there, Mama. Why hadn't I thought about them much before?

"Your mother's sister never spoke to us again. She was very against our marriage. She lives with her family in another village far away. Your mother's brother took over the family house and furniture business."

"Was he against your marriage?"

"No, I don't think so," said Papa. "They wrote letters."

"Why didn't he ever visit?" Amil asked.

"He is a very private person. And maybe his other sister didn't want him to. I'm not sure. Too much time went by and we lost touch."

"How could that be? Time just went by?" Amil said.

I bit my lip. Even though I was desperate for these answers, I wanted Amil to stop asking questions. If he irritated Papa, he would stop talking.

"These things happen," Papa said, and waved his hand. Then he lowered his voice "You must know that the way I feel is very dangerous now. Do not talk about your mother with other people."

"But maybe if people know the truth about us, about our mother, it would be a good thing and we wouldn't have to be on a side," said Amil. His voice sounded small and tight. My mouth fell open. I couldn't believe Amil was saying this. He told me it was ridiculous when I said it.

"No," Papa shouted at him. "You don't understand. You could be killed! You can't change people's minds now. It's the only way to protect yourself. When we leave for the new India, things will be better, I hope."

Papa's eyes moved away from us and on to his cup.

"Papa?" Amil asked. "When are we leaving?"

"I'm not sure. Soon, but that's enough for now. I want to enjoy my tea," Papa said, his mouth returning to a closed, straight line, and picked up his cup.

The new India. Suddenly all those feelings I had about going to a new and beautiful place seemed wrong. I didn't want the new India. I wanted the old one that was my home. Tears started to build up, but I wiped my face hard and pressed on my eyes for a second.

What is going to happen to Kazi, Mama? He's the only one who looks at me with happy, loving eyes. No one else looks at me that way, not even Papa. When Papa looks at us, his eyes are always looking back inside his head at his own thoughts. He sees and he doesn't see. Amil is my twin brother. Looking at him is like looking at myself. Dadi is all full of busy tasks and making noises with her teeth. If you're listening, you must make sure that Kazi comes with us. Jinnah and Nehru can't take him away from us. It's not fair.

Love, Nisha

August 7, 1947

Dear Mama,

I'm lying here, my belly so full that I must lean back and stretch my legs way out. I have so much to write about, but I want to sleep so badly. There's no moon tonight, but I have a little candle and some matches from the kitchen cupboard that I hide under my pillow so I can see in the dark. Amil is snoring. He always falls asleep quickly, the moment his head touches his pillow. Not me. It takes me a long time, even on a night like this, though it's easier with the diary. After I finish, it's like the part of me that can't fall asleep, the part that's staring at the cracks on the ceiling, wondering and worrying, is emptied in the diary for the night. During the day I fill back up and the pages wait. I like to think you're holding my thoughts for me until I can tend to them again. I'm too sleepy now. It will have to wait. Good night, Mama.

Love, Nisha

August 7, 1947

Dear Mama,

I fell asleep for a few hours and woke with a start. I don't know why. Then I started thinking about the party and these thoughts won't leave me alone until I tell you. Amil is breathing so deeply, only an earthquake would wake him. I wish I could sleep like that.

Most of the party was wonderful, until the last part. I think you would have been so proud of Papa.

I will remember it forever. We made so much food, we could have another party tomorrow. Rice, lots of different curries, dal, kebab, poori, paratha, samosa, mango pickle, gulab jamun, and rasmalai. It was so much work that Dadi didn't mind I was in the kitchen all day helping Kazi with everything. I made the sai bhaji all by myself. He let me use his mortar and pestle to ground up the cumin, coriander, and ginger. I curdled the milk and tied the cheese cloths for the rasmalai. I made bowls of thick raita with cucumbers from the garden. I chopped onions with a stick in my teeth and didn't even cry.

My fingernails were stained yellow from the turmeric when I dressed in my best salwar kameez, and I didn't even try to wash it off. The kameez has a dark pink and green design with gold trim and a pink salwar to go with it. I haven't worn it in a year, but it still fits. It even has a pink chiffon dupatta with little gold tassels that I can wrap around my neck or drape over my head. I stared at myself in the bathroom mirror for a long time. Mama, I've always thought I looked like Papa and Amil looks like you, but today I could see you in my face, in the curve of my mouth when I smiled. I have a little space between my two front teeth just like you do. I wondered why I was just noticing this. Then I put a little of Dadi's kohl on my eyes to make them more like yours and hoped Papa wouldn't notice. If he did, he was too busy to say anything. Many girls wear kohl, but Papa is very strict about those things. Sometimes I think he forgets I'm a girl.

I haven't ever seen Papa move around so much in our house the way he did today. It was the strangest thing. He straightened furniture and dusted. He tasted all the food to make sure it was seasoned properly. He took out a small red and blue woven carpet I never knew we had and placed it at the front door. He also asked Amil to sweep the floors and wash the windows. Amil didn't complain. Papa even set out candles and lit incense.

When everything was ready we stood by the door and people began to tumble in with wide smiles, wearing their best clothes, arms full of flowers and sweets, rose perfume floating in the air. So many people came, many of our neighbors, my uncles, my aunties, my cousins, Dr. Ahmed and his family.

How are you my dear? Look how big you are! How beautiful you've gotten! How are you doing in school? Are you eating enough? The aunties asked, their questions flying out for me to grab hold of. But I didn't catch any of them. I just smiled and let their words rush past me, but they never seemed to mind. I received lots of wet lipsticked-kisses on my cheeks, which made me feel disgusted and loved as I turned to secretly rub off their marks. I wonder what it feels like to have words come out of your mouth that you don't even have to think about, that you don't have to take five deep breaths before you even shape your mouth around the first letter and push the word out with your tongue.

When Dr. Ahmed arrived, he presented me and Amil with two tiny gold coins. He closed them in our palms and told us to always be well. His eyes seemed moist. I quickly looked down at my feet, pressed my hands together, and bowed my head. Amil did the same, thanked him, and we ran off to put the coins in our room.

My cousins and the neighborhood children crowded around me and Amil until we took them outside to the best spot for cricket. The boys played a match while the girls sat and wove necklaces out of the flowering weeds around us. We took turns running back into the house for food and drinks and then out again, sometimes bringing a napkin full of snacks. Every time I went in, I saw Papa sitting on the floor, surrounded by men, talking, laughing, eating, and smoking. Again, just like when I was at the market, I wondered how anything could be wrong if our neighborhood could still have a party like this? Kazi stayed in the kitchen, only coming out to refill a bowl of food. I poked my head in, but he shooed me out quickly.

Once I was waved over to sit with my aunties while I ate a samosa. I ate it slowly, savoring the crispy outside tingling with the tart green chutney I dipped it in. One of my aunties told me I needed to fatten myself up and have more food. Another gently reached over and pinched my cheek. But mostly they talked to one another about what flowers were growing well this time of year and who was having a baby and who was getting married. Nobody talked about the changes happening all around us. I looked into their busy, glittery eyes as they spoke, wrists jingling with bangles. What were they really thinking, Mama?

Outside, Amil was awful at cricket as usual, his skinny arms barely able to make a solid hit or throw, but this was just a party game, nothing serious. We girls put on our flower necklaces. I laughed out loud as we held hands and danced in circles. When my cheeks felt warm and rosy, my head a little dizzy from the dancing, my belly happily stuffed with samosas, I whispered to my cousin Malli, who had her arm around my shoulders, "I'll miss you when we go. But maybe we'll still live close."

"Go where?" she said, and stopped dancing. Then all the girls stopped dancing and stared at me. This is what usually happens when I talk, the exact opposite of what I want to happen. When Amil talks, he usually has to yell over people and say things again and again to get anyone to pay attention.

"The new India," I murmured.

"What do you mean?" she said, looking alarmed.

I thought everyone knew more than I did. I wondered if I had told a terrible secret. I wiped my forehead and shrugged. She waited for me to say something else, but I couldn't. My mouth pressed closed. My body felt limp and tired. She cocked her head to the side. I felt my courage to speak go out like a flame.

"Tell me," she said again in a soft voice. But it didn't matter how quietly she said anything. "Tell me," she said louder.

Sabeen suddenly spoke up. "Don't you know? All the Hindus and Sikhs have to leave. We are supposed to stay," she stated plainly. She looked at the other girls, but no one said anything more.

Malli looked like she might cry and ran inside calling her mother. I stood frozen. The other girls watched me for a few more seconds to see if I was going to say anything else, and when I didn't, they resumed their dance without me in it, but not with the same energy. I decided to go inside. Maybe a sweet would make me feel better.

I walked in and saw Malli sitting next to Deepu Aunty, in the corner. Aunty was rubbing her back, soothing her. They both looked upset. Then I saw Papa talking with Rupesh Uncle and my other uncle, Raj. They spoke excitedly, waving their arms around. Then Rupesh Uncle hugged Papa hard and walked over to Malli and Aunty. They got up, said a few goodbyes to others, not me, and slipped out the door. Raj Uncle's family followed. Maybe they didn't see me, or maybe they didn't want to see me. Was it the last time I would ever see them?

When they left, it was like a plug being pulled. The joy started to drain out. A frantic feeling started to grow, travel through my body, as if I was supposed to find that plug, put it back in, and stop whatever was happening. I wanted to go back to the beginning of the party.

I wondered what Papa was saying to people, but I didn't dare go near. There was more hugging. When Dr. Ahmed left, he and Papa held on to each other's arms for a long time, saying quiet things and nodding. Papa stood at the door silently for a minute after he left and wiped his eyes. Was he crying? I couldn't tell. Papa turned and saw me hiding near the kitchen. He waved me over to the door. I reluctantly came. One by one, our last guests gave Papa, Dadi, me, and Amil long hugs that started to make my shoulders hurt. My flower necklace got crushed. Many people whispered in my ear things like "be safe" and "be strong." I had known it all along, that it was a good-bye party, but now I felt the truth sink down into my stomach like a pile of coal.

After everyone went home, Amil and I lay on our beds quietly.

"I told Malli that we were leaving, and she didn't know. I thought everyone knew," I spoke into the balmy darkness. I could still smell the scent of spices, perfume, and incense swirling around in the air.

"I did, too," Amil said.

"I think I ruined the party when I told her."

"It was already ruined," Amil said. His words were slow and heavy.

"What do you mean?" I asked him.

"I don't know. It just seemed so sad from the beginning."

"Really? I didn't think so."

Amil said nothing back and closed his eyes. When his breathing grew deep and rhythmic, I got up and tiptoed out of the room. My heart pounded. I was supposed to stay in my room after bedtime. I always heard Papa and Dadi, and sometimes even Kazi, clinking around, and usually it was enough to comfort me, but tonight I needed to see someone. I peered around the corner and saw Papa sitting at the table alone drinking a cup of tea, staring out before him. I walked closer and stood near the table facing him.

"I can't sleep," I said.

He narrowed his eyes at me and was silent for a few moments. "Neither can I," he finally said, and patted the table. "Get some warm milk."

I relaxed and went into the kitchen. I lit the stove and warmed some milk in a little pan with cardamom seed. When it was steamy, I poured it into a teacup and came to the table. We sat quietly.

"Did you enjoy the party?" Papa finally asked me.

I nodded. Then I took a deep breath and said, "I'm sorry I told Malli we were leaving."

Papa looked at me and took a sip of his tea.

"It's time Malli knew. You're old enough now to understand and so is Malli."

I nodded, Mama, but I don't really understand. It's one thing to understand facts and another thing to understand why those facts are facts. I sat for a little while more with Papa. It was strange to be alone with him, and I realized I hardly ever was. I studied his face—his wide nose, his round cheeks, the lines in his forehead, his eyes squinting at his heavy thoughts as he sipped. I couldn't imagine Papa as a child, carefree and playful. It was like he was born an adult, a father, a doctor.

There was one thing I did understand. I would have memories of life here in Mirpur Khas and memories of life in the new India. My childhood would always have a line drawn through it, the before and the after.

Love, Nisha

August 8, 1947

Dear Mama,

It's the day after the party, but it's like nothing has changed. Papa went to work. Amil and I wandered around trying to think of stuff to do. I helped Kazi cook. Sometimes Dadi would ask us to sweep or wash or fold or put away. After we'd go out and sit on a blanket in the garden to draw and read. I've been reading some of Papa's medical books. Papa likes it, I can tell. He stands over me to see what part I'm reading, nods, and walks away. Maybe he thinks I'll be a doctor one day even though I hate blood, and bad smells, and the actual insides of bodies.

I just want to know what people are thinking. Maybe if I understand how the body works, if I know what every part of it looks like inside, I'll understand more. I study the heart, the ventricles, the arteries, the bones, the liver, the kidneys, the spleen, the lungs, the blood that runs through the veins. I study the brain, the weird coiled blob that holds everyone's secrets. Is it the brain that makes me quiet sometimes, that makes Amil see letters every which way? Is it the brain that makes people love and hate? Or is it the heart?

Love, Nisha

August 15, 1947

Dear Mama,

It's happening now. Sorry I haven't written you for six whole days. The last few days have blended into one. There has been packing and Dadi trying to hide her crying and lots of stern explaining from Papa. Amil keeps running from Papa, to Dadi, to Kazi asking questions. I am silent. No words of mine could change anything. Papa tells us with change, good and bad things will come. At midnight, while we were sleeping, India became independent from British rule. At the same moment, Pakistan, a new country, now exists. Where I live is not called India anymore.

I'm still not sure what it means to be free from British rule. Papa says they have ruled over India for almost two hundred years. I don't feel British at all. English children from the books or newspapers I've seen don't look like I do. They have light skin. They wear different clothes. I know Papa drinks English tea and has English biscuits. I know that there is a British guard who stands outside the Mirpur Khas City Hospital. I know that we have British furniture in our bungalow, like the upholstered wooden chairs in the sitting room and our large oval dining table and English china. I also know that the British aren't going to be the rulers anymore and I guess we don't like British people telling us what to do. Will Papa drink different tea? Will the guard leave? Will we have to give back the chairs and table?

Pakistan was for the Muslims and everybody else will go to India, which isn't here anymore. I wondered if any Hindus were staying anyway. Amil asked Papa that same question, but Papa says it's not safe and the fighting will probably get worse. All non-Muslims in

Mirpur Khas have to leave and the Muslims in the new India are coming here. Papa says it was a group decision between Lord Mountbatten for the British, Jinnah for the Muslims, and Nehru for everyone else. They all agreed to the partition. Amil asked if Gandhi was part of that group. Papa said that Gandhi wants a united India, that we are all Indian no matter what faith we follow. But it doesn't matter now, he says. The decisions have been made, and we must make the best of it and go peacefully.

So as of today, the ground I'm standing on is not India anymore. And Kazi is supposed to live in one place and we're supposed to leave and find a new home. Is there a Muslim girl sitting in her house right now who has to leave her home and go to a new country that's not even called India? Does she feel confused and scared, too?

But here is the question that is most on my mind. I'm afraid to say it, even afraid to write it down. I don't want to think about the answer, but my pencil needs to write it anyway: If you were alive, would we have to leave you because you are Muslim? Would they have drawn a line right through us, Mama? I don't care what the answer is. We came from your body. We will always be a part of you, and this will always be my home even if it's called something else.

Love, Nisha

August 16, 1947

Dear Mama,

I saw the newspaper on Papa's desk. There were pictures of people celebrating on both sides, India and Pakistan. But it's still two sides of the same country to me. I don't feel like celebrating. The headlines said *Birth of India's Freedom*, and *Nation Wakes to New Life*, and *Frenzied Enthusiasm in Bombay*. But all births are not happy. Like me and Amil. Ours wasn't. We lived and you died. It must have been a terrible day for Papa when we were born. I wonder if he even loved us then. I wonder if it's hard to love us all the way now. It's like India—a new country is born, but my home is dying.

Nobody is celebrating freedom in our house. I

must pack my things. I must leave all my books. Our rugs and tables and bookshelves and Papa's desk and most of the stuff in the kitchen except for a few pots and pans and dry food are staying behind. I heard Papa telling Dadi there are riots everywhere and, if we don't leave, we could be killed or taken to a refugee camp. Who would do this? Our neighbors? The kids we went to school with? The merchants at the market? Patients who Papa treated at the hospital? My teacher? Dr. Ahmed? Papa says that everyone is killing one another now, Hindus, Muslims, Sikhs. Everyone is to blame. He says that when you separate people into groups, they start to believe that one group is better than another. I think about Papa's medical books and how we all have the same blood, and organs, and bones inside us, no matter what religion we're supposed to be.

I went into my room to pack. Amil had already finished. He only packed his paper, pencils, and some clothes. We are allowed to take one sack each. We will take the train to the border tomorrow and then change trains to go to Jodhpur, our new home. Papa said a carriage will take us to the train. I put in my clothes, three pencils to write with, this diary, and all of your jewelry that I keep inside a little silk spice sack. Papa says I can't wear it anymore, that people might try to take it. I put in Dr. Ahmed's gold coin, too. I also put in a pinch of dirt from our garden so I'll always have a bit of the ground you walked on, a piece of my India.

Love, Nisha

August 17, 1947

Dear Mama,

It's definite. Papa told us this morning that Kazi is not coming with us tomorrow. I kept hoping there was a way, but Papa says it's too dangerous and Kazi says he can't.

Couldn't he just say he's Hindu and dress in Papa's clothes?

Tonight we had a quick dinner of paratha and dal, since most things are packed or given away. Kazi made my favorite kind of dal with red lentils and

mustard seeds that pop in my mouth. While he pre-
pared it, I sat on the wooden stool swinging my legs.
I didn't want to help, not tonight. I knocked on the
counter so he'd look at me, not sure if I could say his
name out loud.

He looked up as he crushed the cumin with his
mortar.

"What is it, Nishi?" he asked.

I looked down and bit my lip, hard. "You have to
come with us," I murmured, and my voice broke. The
tears started to fall. I wiped them quickly away.

"It's okay, Nishi," he said. "I've been crying, too," he
said, handing me a small towel.

I looked at him in surprise.

"I have, but I could make you all a target if I come.
People think they are defending themselves, standing
up for their people, but it's all out of fear," he told me.

"How would people know, if you dressed in Papa's
clothes and said you were Hindu?" I asked him, my
voice stronger now.

"People have a way of finding out these things. I'd
have to change my name. I'd need fake paperwork. It's
too dangerous."

"So you aren't coming with us because of fear," I said without thinking.

"You should speak more, Nishi. You're a wise child. Probably because you've spent so much time listening instead of talking."

My face felt hot, burning.

"Yes, it's fear. Mostly for you, not me. If something happened to any of you because I was there, I wouldn't be able to live with myself."

I squeezed my hands into fists and tried to keep the tears back. Kazi went on. He told me he would look after the house, that maybe we might come back someday. He didn't look at me anymore and poured the cumin powder into a little bowl. He washed the mortar and pestle and dried it. I sat quietly and watched, my throat feeling thick and scratchy. Then he held out the mortar and pestle and asked me to take it.

I shook my head. If I took it, that would mean I was really saying good-bye. I couldn't lose him. I wouldn't.

He pressed it into my hands and told me to think of him every time I used it. "Don't forget what I've taught you. Making food always brings people to-gether," he said.

I ran my hands over the smooth white marble. The center of the mortar bowl was stained a golden brown from all the spices that had been crushed in there. I put it back on the counter and shook my head. I felt my body shaking. He pushed it toward me again.

"Even if you don't take it," he went on to say, "I will have to stay and you will have to leave. It won't change anything."

I grabbed it and ran out of the kitchen. I wrapped it tight in a shawl and stuffed it into my bag before Papa could see it and tell me not to carry such a heavy thing.

We were very quiet at dinner and after, as Kazi was cleaning up, Amil ran over to him and hugged him hard. Papa looked up with glassy eyes and stared at Kazi. Then Papa shooed Amil away. I couldn't hug Kazi. I was too sad. I got up and followed Amil who ran outside to the garden. He sat on the end of the rows of spinach and tore at the leaves, stuffing a few in his mouth.

"Who's going to eat all this spinach? Kazi won't be able to," he said to me.

We sat quietly for a minute or two. The sun had

started to set. I could hear the rustling of birds and insects and other creatures settling into the evening. Some going to sleep, some waking.

"Do you think we'll ever see Kazi again?" Amil asked.

I didn't want to answer either way. I was afraid we wouldn't. But that would be the same as Kazi dying, wouldn't it?

"I don't even believe we're leaving," I said. Then I whispered, "I feel like we're leaving Mama, too. Because she was here in this house. But our new home. She won't be there."

"She isn't here either, no matter what stupid stories you've made up in your head."

"I'm not making up stories!" I yelled back at him. Amil jumped. Then I started to cry again and Amil looked away. He suddenly got up and ran back into the house. He was probably scared of me. I felt ashamed and lonely. Mama, if you were here, would you have sat next to me and held me? Would you have loved me more than all of them?

Amil came running back with a handkerchief and held it out to me. My body relaxed. I thanked him, relieved he hadn't left me all alone. I took the kerchief and wiped my nose and eyes, my chest feeling a little lighter.

"We never knew her. What's the point of thinking about her?" Amil said.

I nodded. It was okay that he felt that way. He must love you deep inside, but I kind of like having you all to myself. I feel like I do know you, because I know myself and you made me. I'm going to take you with me, closed up tight in this diary and in the little pouch with the dirt and your jewelry.

"I do sometimes."

"You do think about Mama?" I said.

"A little. She looks so pretty in her picture. I bet she would have been different from—" but he stopped talking.

"Different from what?" I asked. But I knew what he was going to say, different from Papa. See Mama, he does love you. It's just harder for him to say it. I wonder sometimes if Amil feels things as big as I do. He uses his body more to move, to talk, so everything isn't locked up inside the way it is with me. Sometimes I wish I were Amil. Is that strange, Mama, wanting to be a boy? It just seems like it would be easier. But then I guess Papa wouldn't like me as much.

Amil sat back down next to me and leaned against my shoulder. I could feel the warmth from his body that was always moving. He sat very still, though, as we watched the sun go down over our garden for the last time.

Love, Nisha

August 18, 1947

Dear Mama,

I'm writing this only by moonlight under my mosquito net, so forgive me if it is messy. I can barely see what I'm putting down, but I have a talent. I can write without seeing. We tried to leave this morning. The sun hadn't even come up yet. Kazi stayed in his cottage. Before bed Kazi came to say one last good-bye to us and told us he was going to stay in his cottage when we left in the morning because it was safer.

"Until I see you again," he said, and hugged us both. I couldn't cry. I felt like I was a dry leaf floating in the wind wondering where I'd land. I just nodded and floated away from him. If I said good-bye, then it would be a real good-bye, a forever good-bye.

Amil once drew a picture of Kazi. It was of him in the kitchen with a towel thrown over his shoulder, chopping vegetables. Kazi looks very serious in the picture, his eyes squinting, his lips pressed together. I went into Amil's stacks of drawings that he keeps in the corner of our room and tried to find it, but I couldn't.

Dadi quietly woke us and we had yogurt and day-old roti without talking. Somehow everyone knew that this was not a time for talking, as if the loud words placed in the fragile air would break something. There is so much you can understand from a person's face— the way they stare or nod or press their lips together or turn their heads to the side in a certain way. So much talking happens with no words.

We gathered our belongings and spoke with our eyes, our nods, our shrugs, our pointing fingers. I had my bag, Amil had his. We had bedrolls rolled up and strapped to our backs. Papa had loaded what he could in the covered horse carriage, Dadi's things, his clothes, two bedrolls, a mosquito net, his medicine bag, some books, all the food and jugs of water, some pots and pans and cups, and a wrapped painting of yours. Papa didn't show us the painting, but I know all the sizes. I think it's my favorite one of a hand holding an egg. I always wondered if you had painted someone's actual hand or if you imagined it. It looks like a woman's hand. Was it Dadi's? Was it yours? Why was it holding an egg? When I saw it in the carriage, I felt so happy. More of you would be coming with us. I also have your jewelry. I have the dirt from our home, and I have this diary.

We planned to take a carriage to the train, and we had to leave before dawn so no one would see us leaving. Papa had heard about fighting when people left. Raj and Rupesh Uncle left days ago by train and are now on the other side. They're finding us a place to live so when we get there, we will have a home. Papa says we are very lucky and there will be many people scattered with no homes.

The hospital made Papa stay longer than he wanted to until a new doctor could come. A Muslim doctor is coming to fill Papa's post and work with Dr. Ahmed. He will move into our home. I guess Kazi needs to stay and cook for him. I didn't want to think about it. When Papa came home on his last day at the hospital, he only said one thing. "I hope he saves more than I did." Then he went into his room and didn't come out for the rest of the evening.

I kept my bag close to me because I didn't want Papa or Dadi to feel how heavy it was because of the mortar and pestle. When we were packing yesterday, Papa made Amil bring the Mahabharata book and only a few scraps of paper and two pencils. Amil was furious that he had to take the book instead of his drawings, but Papa told him he couldn't throw fits like a child anymore, that he was almost a man now. Amil stopped yelling and swallowed. Then he shook his head and walked away. He went to our room and put all his drawings into one pile. He walked into the kitchen with them and begged Kazi to burn them in the stove. He said he didn't want to leave them for anyone else to take.

Kazi took them, laid them on the table carefully, and promised Amil he'd keep them safe. He said if he left, he'd take them with him.

"No," Amil said. "I'm almost a man." Then he grabbed them and thrust them into the lit coal stove. He was so quick, Kazi couldn't stop him. Amil ran outside. I stood staring at Kazi and I felt the tears come again, but I wiped them away and walked over to the stove. I watched all Amil's drawings burn into ash. Kazi watched them, too. He put his arm around me as we watched.

"He'll draw more. He'll make new drawings at your new home," he said, trying to make me feel better, but for some reason I felt like I had been stabbed in the heart.

"Amil," I said, later in the day while Amil sat on the floor folding and unfolding a blank piece of paper. "Why?"

"They will burn here, so I might as well be here when they do."

"But Kazi said he'd keep them. Nobody's going to burn them."

Amil just shook his head angrily. "We don't know. Maybe someone will burn our house to the ground," he said in a low voice.

"That's not going to happen," I said. "A new family is coming here."

"I'd rather it burn," Amil said to me, his eyes dark and wild.

"You don't mean that," I said. But I know he did.

Amil just rocked back and forth, unfolding and folding his paper. I sat with him for a while and watched his fingers furiously climb over the paper. I could see the anger leak out of him a little bit. I took the soft, wrinkled piece from him. He let me.

"Let's go be with Kazi," Amil suddenly said, and got up quickly. I could tell he was trying to shake off his feelings. He didn't like to be angry. I loved that about him, that he really wanted to be happy. Sometimes I like to hold on to my upsets, like if I let them go I'm admitting they weren't that important, but Amil isn't like that. When we fight, he's usually the first to apologize, the first to lift us out of our hurt. But in the last few days, I could see an anger always behind his eyes, smoldering.

I wasn't sure I wanted to be with Kazi, but I followed. We sat with Kazi for the rest of the day while he packed up the kitchen and made food packages for us. He handed us pieces of radishes and peppers to snack on as he worked. Then we began to help him, scrubbing pots and tying up bags of rice and lentils that Kazi would either pack for us or take with him to his cottage. It felt better to work, to keep my body moving. If I worked in the kitchen I could pretend none of this was happening. We were just making dinner, like always. I wondered if I pretended enough, would it become the truth?

Then this morning while we shuffled outside in the cool air and finished loading up the carriage, we heard the sound of someone running toward us. I think I heard it first because I looked toward the sound and then everyone else looked. The scrape and scratch of sandals hitting dirt moved closer, grew louder. Papa pushed the three of us back in the house. "Go," he said in a harsh whisper, pushing at our backs. "Hide in the pantry." Dadi grabbed our arms and pulled us inside. Someone was coming for us.

We crouched in the pantry again, trying not to breathe. It was a lot emptier now. Dadi moved her lips slightly, murmuring prayers to herself. I could hear the low buzz of men's voices, but they didn't sound angry or scary. I was worried someone was coming to hurt Papa, but I held on to the sound of low voices, Papa's and another man's that sounded familiar but I couldn't place him. Maybe it was someone telling us we didn't have to leave, that this was all a big mistake.

I felt Dadi's warm, misty breath on my shoulder. Amil grabbed my hand. It was cold and dry. Mine was hot and sweaty. We waited for a long time.

Suddenly someone threw open the pantry door letting the first morning sun stream into our blinking, terrified eyes.

"We can't go today." It was Papa. I let my breath out. I wondered if that meant we weren't going at all. A little spark of hope teased at me.

"Why?" Dadi asked.

"That was cousin Nikhil. He said he heard terrible things about some trains trying to cross the border. They've decided to stay longer. But we can't."

"What terrible things?" Amil said, his voice curious and hungry. I wanted to hear it, too, Mama. I wanted to hear something so bad and terrible it would make me want to run away and never look back.

"I told you. People are being killed," Papa said in a flat voice, as if he were telling us to go to sleep. He didn't say what people, where, and how.

Dadi started to murmur prayers out loud now. We all stayed crouched in the closet. Papa yelled at her. "Ma!" She stopped and quietly pressed her lips together.

"What will we do?" she asked. "It's at least a hundred miles to the border."

"We will leave on foot tomorrow. It's too light now," Papa said. "We need to stay here one more day. We can stop at Rashid Uncle's on the way. I'll arrange for a messenger to notify him. It's about halfway."

"Rashid!" Dadi said.

"Rashid Uncle?" Amil asked, and my eyes lit up. I had heard the name before. It had to be your brother, Mama. I prayed Papa would answer Amil.

"Hush," Papa said. "You all must listen to everything I tell you now. Tonight we will sleep at Kazi's, so it looks like we're not here. The riots are getting closer."

"But," Amil said, and Papa put his hand up to stop him.

"Amil," Papa said sternly, "enough."

My shoulders sank. Then I felt the pang of guilt I always did when I wanted Amil to push Papa for answers. I wanted to see if I was right about Rashid Uncle. We had hardly ever been inside Kazi's cottage. Kazi only went there to sleep and spend his Sunday there, his day off. We were not to bother him then. But a few times when we were bored, Amil and I didn't listen and visited Kazi anyway. Once, about a year ago, Amil found a strange tomato in the garden. It looked like three tomatoes stuck together.

"Let's show Kazi," he said, holding it up, then balancing it on his head.

"We can't," I answered, and took it from him so it wouldn't fall and bruise. I wanted to know what a three-headed tomato tasted like.

"You always listen to the rules," Amil said, and crossed his arms.

"Well, you never do," I shot back. "And that's why you make Papa upset."

Immediately I felt bad for what I said. That wasn't really why Papa got frustrated with Amil. It was because Papa didn't understand why Amil was so bad at school and was worried he'd never become a doctor.

But Amil didn't get mad at me. He just sighed. "Why don't you talk this way to anyone else? You leave all the rule breaking to me. You like it that way."

I didn't know what to say. Then he took the tomato from me and ran to Kazi's house before I could do anything. I followed after him, stunned, wondering if I did like it that way. But I think he liked it that way, too. I felt the things he couldn't feel and he said the things I couldn't say, except to him. That's how it worked.

Kazi never let us stay long—just took our gift and shooed us off. I don't know what he did there all day long on Sundays. Mama, my eyes are drooping, I will finish when I can.

Love, Nisha

August 19, 1947

Dear Mama,

There are two rooms in Kazi's cottage, a front room with a small kitchen, and a little table with two chairs in the middle. Then there's the back room with his bed, a rug, a chair in the corner, and a small chest of drawers. There's a small tapestry that hangs on the wall of the front room and that's it.

We spent yesterday staying in the back room being quiet, reading and drawing and hoping no one came to hurt us. Our house stood dark and empty. Now we had no carriage and could only take what we could carry on our backs. We would have to leave your painting with Kazi. Papa was worried about the water. Dadi said it was too heavy, that she didn't need much. Papa made us take extra anyway.

We sat on the floor with our backs against the walls. Amil and I sat on one side, Papa and Dadi on the other. It was strange, not being allowed to speak. Suddenly all I wanted to do was talk. I wonder if that's how normal children feel all the time. I wanted to ask how Papa felt about leaving this house and the hospital. I wanted to ask him if he was scared. I wanted to ask him if we were ever coming back. Amil and I had short, whispering conversations, but then Papa would put his finger over his mouth and an hour would go by and we wouldn't speak. My mouth itched with words. Would people really hear us talking? But I didn't dare cross Papa.

I kept hoping we would somehow get to stay. We would sleep in Kazi's cottage for a few days and then quietly move back into our house. The hope I felt made the hours a little shorter and pulled me along. Kazi sat outside guarding the house. I longed to sit with him.

Kazi and Papa made a plan. Kazi would knock three times on the door if he sensed danger, and we were all supposed to climb out the back window and run to the garden shed behind Kazi's cottage. I couldn't imagine Papa and Dadi climbing out the window. Thinking about it made the corners of my mouth turn up and twitch, even though I knew I shouldn't smile at such things.

Every few hours, Dadi would give us a bit of roti and lentils to eat with a few radishes and a slice of mango. I saved my mango slices wrapped in a cloth napkin so I could eat them all at once before bed. Every time I ate a mango slice, I felt happy for that moment. The more slices, the longer the happiness. When I got my mat ready for sleep, I still tasted the syrupy mango juice on my tongue. Amil whispered in my ear.

"This was the longest day of my life," he said. I nodded hard and leaned against his bony shoulder. Dadi sat cross-legged and hummed prayers very softly. Papa did stretches. If I thought the quiet was hard, Amil must have been ready to explode.

I tried to read, but I couldn't concentrate on anything. I was waiting for a chance to talk to Kazi. I was also listening for rioters, for the scrape of shoes on the dirt, the first sounds of yelling growing closer, or the crackle of a torch. I listened for Kazi's knocks. I thought of you, too, Mama. I thought about your painting of the hand with the egg. Maybe you painted it when you were pregnant with us, your belly big, all the windows open, the breeze blowing through the house. Maybe when you painted that picture you were happier than you'd ever been, would ever be.

We left this morning when the sun was just starting to peek through the clouds. Amil looked at me nervously. He bit his lip. Dadi patted our hands. "It will be okay," she said. "Your Papa will get us to the other side."

I didn't want to go to the other side. It reminded me of dead people. The people in the hospital that Papa couldn't save. You, Mama. You are on the other side. We're still here.

"Where's Kazi?" Amil whispered to Papa as we filed out the door.

"One good-bye is enough, I think," Papa said in a hoarse tone. Then we walked out on the dirt path past our house. I couldn't look at it straight on, only out of the corner of my eye. I wanted to see Kazi's face one last time. Would he be mad at me because I never properly said good-bye? I should have. How stupid of me to think I'd have another chance. I pressed the lump of the mortar and pestle in my bag. This is all I was left with. I cried softly, making no sound. Only my shoulders shaking. Then I swallowed it all down.

We didn't walk through town. It was too dangerous. We walked through shaggy fields of prickly grasses until we found a clearer path toward the desert. There were people behind and in front of us. Some people had oxcarts filled high with belongings. Some people rode camels. We carried less than everyone else around us except for the water. We each had a large jug that would last us a few days before we would need to fill it. Papa carried two.

Papa told us before we left to keep our heads down, not to talk to anyone no matter who they were. Dadi walked close to me. She told me I must keep myself as covered as I could with my shawl, that I'm bigger now and strange men can't be trusted. I didn't tell Dadi this, but I only trust four people in the world anyway. I trust Papa, Dadi, Amil, and Kazi. And you Mama, I trust you.

It feels like we're really in a story now. I've heard

about stories like these, about people who flee their homes in a war with nothing but the clothes and food on their backs. Now that's who we are, even though there's not a war here, but it's like a war. It seems almost like a made-up war. It makes each footstep I take feel numb, like my foot isn't actually touching the ground, like I'm not in my body. We had to leave our chess set. We also had to leave my old doll, Dee. Deepu Aunty gave it to me when I was two, so I called the doll Dee to remind me of her. While I walked I thought about Dee, thought about her frayed orange and gold sari and the red color painted on her tiny lips. She even had little gold earrings dangling from her ears and a green jeweled bindi on her forehead. I suddenly missed her so much that my chest hurt, even though I hadn't played with Dee since I was ten. She had sat in the corner of my side of the room to keep watch over me and Amil. Now she would probably be taken by a new girl who would find her.

We walked all day carrying our packs. Dadi couldn't walk that fast, so we went slowly. Papa said we had to cover at least ten miles a day, more if we could, and it should take about four hours, but with breaks it would probably be closer to five or six. Today, our first day, we walked seven hours slowly with breaks, so we probably did around fifteen miles. Papa told us we could only have a small drink of water every hour, which was hard, but I only sipped when Papa told us to. I saw Amil sneaking a sip or two, but I didn't say anything.

Tonight, Papa found us a place next to a big rock near clumps of desert brush. It's kind of like a cave. He didn't want to be too near the other families who were also stopping for the night. Papa likes to be private. At home, we didn't have many people come over. I think his only close friend was Dr. Ahmed. Papa always liked a good party, but he said when he came home after the hospital he just wanted to have some peace and quiet. I think Papa likes to doctor people more than he likes to enjoy people.

We put down our packs and Papa asked us to help him make a fire to keep away the animals and insects. I helped Amil find the right sticks and dead leaves. Then Papa arranged the sticks into a pile with the dried leaves under and lit a match from the box he brought. We all sat and watched the fire eat the leaves, little lapping tongues of flame climbing up the branches. What is it about fire? I can't take my eyes off it.

After a good blaze got going, we warmed our dinner on it, more roti and dal. We only have one pot with us. We have a stack of roti, dal, nuts, dried fruit, and a few bags of dried peas, lentils, and rice.

"Papa," Amil said as he sat on the ground and chewed the dry roti, "is that all the food we have?" He pointed to the bag Papa had carried. "And what if we run out of water?" Amil asked.

"Sip carefully. One drink an hour. We will find a place to fill it back up."

"But what if," Amil started to say. Papa put his finger on his lips.

"One drink an hour," Papa said. "Then we'll find a place to get more."

"In the middle of nothing?" Amil said, swinging his arm around.

Papa glared at him, the light from the fire dancing in his eyes. Amil finally closed his mouth and tended the fire. We checked for scorpions before we sat down. For sleep we had a huge mosquito net that would cover all of us. We needed to keep all our belongings around us, the water, the food, packed tightly in bags and jugs so no animals or people would steal it. We sat for a while around the fire and Dadi sang, her high-pitched voice winding around the air like a butterfly. Amil drew some pictures in the sand with a stick. I didn't want to take my diary out in front of everyone and have Papa see, but it's a habit now, a jumpy feeling that starts in my fingers at night. I was getting that feeling, as darkness fell all around us. I got it out from my bag with my pencil. Papa watched me. I sat back down and started to write.

"What is that, Nisha?" Papa asked.

"My diary," I said in a tiny voice.

"Your diary?" he asked, looking more serious than ever.

My fingers tightened around it. "Kazi gave it to me." Now I know what Kazi meant about writing down all the things the grown-ups won't be able to.

Papa turned his head to the side. His face softened.

"Carry on, then," he said. "But only for a few minutes. You need to rest."

"Yes, Papa," I said, and pressed my pencil to the paper, feeling an electric tingle go up my arm. Then I wrote this.

Love, Nisha

August 20, 1947

Dear Mama,

We're almost out of water. We wouldn't have been so soon, but Amil spilled both his and Dadi's when he tried to carry the two jugs as we packed up this morning. Papa rushed him, telling him he should carry more stuff, that he was almost a man and he should carry Dadi's pack, too. But Amil is so wiry and thin, like a twig you could easily snap in half. I'll bet Dadi could carry more. He did what he was told and as he slung both his and Dadi's pack on his back, and as he was carrying the water jugs and the bedrolls, the jugs fell to the ground, the caps popping off. He didn't even notice at first, but I did. I heard it before I saw it, the water making its *glug, glug* noise, creating a little stream in the dry ground.

"Amil!" I yelled, and ran over to the water. I righted them in the sandy dirt, picked up the caps, and screwed them on quickly, as if moving fast would reverse the damage. Dadi and Papa just stared. I looked up at Amil's face. His mouth hung open. His eyes seemed so wide and helpless, it made my chest hurt. Amil looked at Papa like a little dog about to be kicked. I stood up, holding the almost empty jugs and stood in front of Amil, facing Papa, putting myself between them.

Papa slowly walked toward us. Amil lowered his eyes. Papa's mouth was a straight, thin line. He took the jugs from me and placed them on the ground. Then he silently lined up our other jugs and poured a bit of water from each and evened them out. He handed them back to us.

"Don't spill it again. There's life in here. Treat it like that," he said to Amil with gritted teeth.

Amil kept his head down and nodded. "I'm sorry, Papa." Amil's eyes started to well up. My whole body tensed. Don't cry, Amil, please don't cry, I wished. Amil always cried more than I did. When he was little, he threw lots of tantrums. Papa's face would grow redder and redder as Amil would stomp around and cry because he broke his toy or because Dadi wanted him to sit and finish his dinner.

I always wondered why Amil wasn't scared of Papa like I was, but maybe Amil just couldn't help it. Eventually Papa would take him over his knee and give him a swift hit on his bottom. I knew it didn't really hurt Amil, but it always stopped him. Then Papa's face would collapse, and I could see the regret in his eyes. Amil would stand up, rubbing his behind and sit back down, finally eating, or picking up his toy. But that was years ago. Now Amil knew better than to throw a tantrum.

"Why do you do that?" I once asked him when we were still little enough to be sleeping in the same bed.

"Do what?" Amil asked.

"Make Papa so mad," I said.

"I don't know," Amil said. "Papa really looks at me when I cry."

"He always feels bad when he hits you," I said.

"That's the best part," he had said.

Now I wondered if Papa was mad enough to hit Amil.

"I know you're sorry," was all Papa said. He briskly wiped the tears that started to fall off Amil's face. "Don't cry. Your body needs to hold on to all the water it has."

I was relieved at first as we continued on the trail. But since it was obvious Papa wasn't going to hit him, I felt a burst of anger at Amil. Why couldn't he be more careful? What if we couldn't get water fast enough? But I couldn't say that to Amil. Then I would be like Papa. I don't want to be like Papa. I want to be like you were, Mama, bright and elegant, creating beauty all around you, always kind. That's how I think you were. I can tell by your picture, see it in your eyes. Sometimes I want to be like Kazi, too, safe with my vegetables, spices, and knives in the kitchen, letting the food speak for me. I love Papa, but I don't want to be as serious and sad as he is. And yet I'm probably like Papa the most. Is Amil like you? He's not really elegant, but he's hardly ever sad. Even when he is, the happiness starts to creep in and makes his legs jumpy, his eyes flicker. The happy energy always takes over. For me, it's the opposite.

We tried to drink even less water today, and my throat started to feel dry. My legs began quivering like jelly in the heat. We did find some mango orchards and were able to each grab a bunch for our sacks. Papa said to only eat two a day. I ate one and saved the other for hours, feeling the weight of the mango hit my back as we walked. I finally ate it while we rested by some rocks. I opened the skin with my teeth and pulled the rest of it off with my hand and bit into it. The tangy, thick juice flooded my mouth and I shivered. My teeth sank farther into the soft ripe flesh. After only eating old roti and dal and not much water, it was like eating a fruit custard made out of honey and butter. I wanted to stay there resting, eating mangoes, the breeze blowing on me, almost like I was on holiday, not fleeing the only home I've ever had.

Kazi used to cut up every mango in four pieces, two large ones along the flat side of the big pit in the middle and two small ones along the edges of the pit. Amil and I would fight over the pit, loving to gnaw every bit of fruit off it, the filmy stickiness coating our hands and face.

We've probably walked about eighteen miles or more. We have almost used up our roti and dal, but we still have the dry rice, peas, and lentils. Will Rashid Uncle be kind to us when we arrive there, Mama? It's so strange that we are meeting him now. I'm a little excited and also afraid. Does he hate Papa? All this time, your brother was sixty-five miles away and we never knew it.

My feet are burning even as I sit here and write. I only have one pair of worn leather sandals. I wrap my blisters in cool leaves, but they keep falling off. It still feels so strange to say that the ground where my sore feet step on is not India anymore, but a place called Pakistan. I feel bad for the people who carry many things piled on wagons and their backs. They tried to take too much.

Papa says that once we are over the border he will be able to find work easily, that doctors are always needed. Papa says his brothers will have a home for us in Jodhpur and we will get new things eventually. That's why we barely took anything. I feel lucky that Papa is a doctor. It is the only thing I feel lucky about right now as I try to sleep on my mat, flat against the earth, staring up at the clear sky through the fog of the mosquito net, my throat tasting like dust.

Love, Nisha

August 21, 1947

Dear Mama,

I woke up feeling terrible today. My tongue was stuck to the roof of my mouth. My head pounded. My fingers tingled. When I tried to get up, my arms and legs felt filled with sand.

"Amil," I said, nudging him out of sleep. "Are you feeling strange?"

He mumbled something I couldn't understand. I looked over at Papa and he opened his eyes, and we stared in a way that we never look at each other, not like father and daughter, but simply like two people who are both scared. It made me see Papa suddenly as a person, not just my papa, like a secret door had opened. Then he blinked and it was over.

I crawled over my mat, past Amil, who had fallen back asleep, and I kneeled next to Papa. He put his hand on my shoulder.

"Today we will find water," he said.

I nodded. I wanted to ask him how, but I didn't want him to take his hand away, so I kept silent, but he removed it anyway. I knew we couldn't walk ten miles today without water. We only had a couple sips left in our jugs.

"Is your mouth dry?" Papa asked, sitting up cross-legged on his mat.

"Not really," I murmured in a gravelly voice, turning away from him.

He leaned over and told me to open my mouth. I did as he asked. He squinted in, examining the inside as he pressed his strong fingers against the sides of my face. Then he checked my eyes by lifting up my eyelids. He checked my pulse and lightly pinched the skin on the back of my hand.

"You're okay," he said. "You have another day in you."

Another day and then what? I didn't want to know. Then he went over to Amil. He shook his shoulder, but Amil just moaned with his eyes closed.

"Amil," Papa said loudly.

Amil stirred and turned toward Papa. Dadi came over and squatted by his shoulder.

"Sit up," Papa said sternly.

Amil just blinked at him.

"Sit up," Papa said even louder.

Amil hoisted himself up.

"I feel sick," Amil said in a scratchy voice, his skin dry, his eyes sunken. Papa did all the things he did to me, but he didn't tell Amil he had another day in him.

"Do you have any more water?" Papa asked Amil. Amil shook his head and looked down, shame in his hunched shoulders. He poked his finger into the sandy dirt. He made a line, then another. A picture of a tree suddenly appeared.

Papa gave him his own jug. Amil shook his head.

"Take it. You must," and he thrust it at Amil and swatted his drawing hand.

"Papa," Amil said, taking the jug and shaking it a little. "There's only a sip in here. I don't deserve to finish your water."

"Nonsense," Papa said. "Drink."

Amil drank it in one small gulp. "I'm sorry, Papa," he said, his eyes down on the ground again. He stared at the tree he made.

I went over to my sack, pulled out my last mango and handed it to Amil.

"Did you at least save a mango?" Papa asked Amil. Amil nodded. We all had one left.

"Let's eat them now and we'll find more today. Nisha eat yours. Amil has his own."

"And water," Dadi said. "We must find water." Dadi's voice was also rough and dry.

I looked at her, she appeared pale and sunken around her eyes. Poor Dadi. She should be resting in her favorite chair, singing softly as she mended Papa's shirts. I wouldn't dare say this out loud, but I'm so angry at all the leaders, like Jinnah and Nehru, who were supposed to know better, who were supposed to protect us, who were supposed to make sure things like this didn't happen. I'm even angry at Gandhi for not being able to stop it.

Papa seemed fine. Nothing weakened Papa. In fact, I could never remember him ever being sick, not once. How was that possible? He worked with sickness and disease his whole adult life. Maybe Papa isn't actually human, but a god watching over us. His first name, Suresh, means that he's a ruler of all the gods, the protector, another name for Lord Vishnu. Maybe the worried look in his eye as he examined me and Amil was just for show. Mama, did you ever think that about Papa?

Papa made me take the last of my water. I took one sip and handed the jug to Dadi.

"No, no, sweet child," she said, patting my arm. "I have a bit left."

But I didn't see her sip from her jug. I held the jug toward Papa.

"Drink," he said with stern eyes. So I did. I let it trickle down my throat, but it wasn't enough. I couldn't think of anything more beautiful than buckets of cool, clean water to drink. I ate my mango, but my tongue felt numb and I could barely taste it this time. The thickness of the fruit clung to my lips. It made me yearn for water even more.

We gathered our belongings silently. Normally I was the one who was quiet, my family making noise around me. I liked the noises, Amil's chattering, Dadi's singing or prayers, Papa directing us to do this and that. And Kazi, talking to me in the kitchen. He was the only one in my house who never minded if I didn't answer back, which made me want to talk more. Now the silence covered all of us like mist. We rolled our mats, packed our sacks, and arranged them on our backs. I picked up Dadi's jug when she wasn't looking and shook it. It was empty.

Again I was thankful for the little we had to carry, except for the water. We should have brought a wagonload. I didn't think much about water back home. Badal, the water man, would bring it up the hill to our compound every day from the well. Two leather sacks hung from a big pole across his back. He whistled happily while he walked up the hill, as if he were carrying feathers. I never thought about how heavy it must have been and how lucky we were to have someone bring it to us every day. A wave of shame rippled through the center of my body and made me feel sicker.

Now it feels like water is the only thing I've ever wanted. It isn't only thirst. We haven't washed since we started out. A film of dirt, dust, and sweat coat me like a light covering of hair. My feet are caked with dirt. My teeth feel like apricot skin. It's strange that we don't even have to go to the bathroom anymore. I tried not to think of water as I hoisted my pack and bedroll on my back. I saw a family walking past us in the same direction. I caught a girl's eyes, a few years younger than me, hair and clothing rumpled and dirty. She looked like a small, frightened animal, weighed down by her belongings. I probably looked like that to her.

Papa went ahead to the passing family and leaned his head toward the man of the group, probably speaking in his firm, but gentle doctorly tone that made everything seem all right even when it was terribly wrong. He pointed over to us and turned back. The man wiggled his head and Papa walked back.

"What did you say, Papa?" Amil said, perking up from the moment of mystery.

"I asked for water. I offered him some of our food. But they only have a bit left, with four children. He said there's running water in the next village an hour away."

"How does he know that?" Amil asked.

"Use your head. There's always water in a village."

Amil didn't dare ask any more questions. There was something comforting in the way that Papa was treating Amil. It was the way he always treated him, like an annoying fly. But still, I wish Papa would be nicer to him. Amil is only being all he knows how to be. But I guess Papa is, too. I guess we all are. It's just that some people are better at being than others.

We continued to walk in silence. Papa in the front, me, Amil, then Dadi in a line. There were people up ahead and behind. The dirt felt hard underfoot, and the sun beamed hotly on our bodies drying them out even more. I thought of Kazi and the dried apricots, mangoes, and tomatoes he used to make by hanging thin slices in the sun. I loved the chewiness of the dried fruit, their taste pure and sun-filled, no water to interrupt the flavor. Amil never liked to eat dried fruit. He said it reminded him of the skin of very old people. I thought of us shriveling up like pieces of sliced mangoes.

I slowed my pace a little so Amil could catch up to me. I glanced behind me. His steps didn't have the bounce in them they normally did.

"Are you okay?" I asked him in a whisper, and touched his shoulder.

He nodded. His eyes were dull.

"Really?" I said, my heart speeding up a bit.

He nodded again.

"Because you can tell me if you're not," I said.

"Nisha," he said through gritted teeth, "stop."

So I closed my mouth and walked next to him instead of in front of him.

Papa was ahead of us, since Amil was slow, but I didn't care. I matched my pace with Amil exactly as I could, making sure our feet hit and left the ground at the exact same time. I made it a game and the sound of our footfalls became a beat to a song I heard in my head. It was an old song I heard, a song that Dadi used to sing to us before bed when we were little. Amil used to sing with Dadi, and Dadi would shush him and tell him he wouldn't fall asleep if he sang with her. I remember wishing he would be quiet, too. I just wanted to hear Dadi's voice. Sometimes I would close my eyes and pretend it was you singing to us, Mama. But he would stop only for a few seconds and then start up again. I realized I haven't heard Amil sing in a long time. What I would do to hear him sing now.

Love, Nisha

August 22, 1947

Dear Mama,

We are not good. I can barely write, but if we die here, I want someone to find this. I want someone to know what we went through. There is no answer for our suffering. We are in the rainy season, but it doesn't rain much here. It rained before we started, and now when we need it most, the sky is as dry as our throats. I keep looking up searching for dark clouds, but all I see is blinding blue. Can you send us some rain, Mama?

I also don't think Papa is Vishnu after all. As we got closer to the village, I heard voices, and some yelling and crying. Then I could see a line leading to the pump. We stood at the end of the line and Papa went up ahead.

"Stay here," he said. "I want to see what's going on."

We watched him walk up. The voices grew louder and then we heard a deep yell, and after, a high-pitched scream. The line loosened as everyone tried to see what happened.

Amil started walking closer to see.

"Stay back," Dadi called after him, but he kept walking.

"Amil!" I called, but he wouldn't turn around. I stayed with Dadi, but I wanted to see, too.

"Dadi, can we go closer?" I whispered to her. She squeezed my hand hard until it hurt.

"Don't be foolish," she whispered back, but craned her neck over the crowd. There was more yelling. Amil came back, walking slowly. Normally he would be running and jumping from excitement, but if he felt anything like me, it was hard work just to stand, and I know he felt worse. His eyes had a film covering them, but I could see a frightened spark behind the glaze.

"A man stole water from another man and cut his arm with a knife. Papa's trying to stop the bleeding."

Dadi put her hand to her mouth. I wasn't thinking about the man bleeding. I didn't think about the knife. This is what I thought, Mama—if Papa helped the man, someone would have to give us water. I was jealous of the man who ran off with the water. That's what thirst has done to me.

I wondered if Amil or Dadi was thinking what I was thinking, not that I could ever ask them. And then I saw it a few feet away: a large container on the ground, no one too near it. I could tell the way it sat firmly on the ground that it was heavy, probably filled with water. I started to inch toward it. If I could get a good gulp and quickly give one to Amil and Dadi, we'd be able to go another day. I inched over until I was only a foot away and reached out. I saw feet fly toward me and a man grabbed the jug, dust and dirt rising up. I staggered back and the man growled at me. He actually growled. I recoiled like a cat. Dadi pulled me back in line.

"Nisha, what are you doing? Stand close!" I froze next to her, afraid to move.

We got closer to the pump. Amil was ahead of us, walking slowly. Then I saw Papa, kneeling on the ground by a man, splashes of blood in the dirt. He was wrapping a shirt around the man's wound. The man had his head tipped back, his eyes closed. A woman stood crying over him, a baby on her hip, wiping her eyes with her shawl. The pump ran dry. A man furiously stood pumping and pumping, but nothing came out. Some groups started to walk away.

I eyed the man with Papa and looked around for other water containers. There was one next to the injured man, but he held on to it with his free hand. Other people went up to the pump and tried it, even though the person before got nothing. After Papa finished dressing the man's wound, Papa asked him if we could have a sip of water and pointed toward us. I moved forward, my mouth parted slightly. I imagined the water sliding down my throat. The man eyed me, then Amil and Dadi. He quickly got to his feet. "Not enough," he said, and hobbled away as fast as he could, clutching the container, his wife and baby following.

I wanted to grab the man by the shoulders. We deserved this water! He might have bled to death without Papa's help. Take it, Papa, I wanted to scream, just take it. But instead I cast my eyes down on the blood in the dirt.

Love, Nisha

August 24, 1947

Dear Mama,

I've never really thought about dying before. I mean I've thought about other people dying, but I've never thought about me not actually being here anymore. You think I would have because I've seen many people dying in hospital beds, eyes rolled up to the ceiling, mouths hanging open. I've seen them covered with a sheet when they've passed. I've seen them lying on their funeral beds covered in flowers, being wheeled down the street by their families on the way to crema- tion. I've seen Papa's oldest brother, Vijay Uncle, who died of a heart attack two years ago, covered in white cloth, orange and yellow flowers placed carefully around his lifeless body before his cremation, looking as peaceful as someone napping.

But yesterday morning I thought we were all going to die. Amil first, then Dadi, then me, then Papa. That's the order of how I thought it would happen. We would just flicker out like flames in the quiet night. My mind filled with inky dark colors, like someone had locked me in a box. Just five days ago we were sleeping in Kazi's cottage. Kazi. What was he doing right now? It hurt to think about it.

We were too weak to walk much after we left the village, so we found a shady place under some trees and lay there close together. Every once in a while, Papa would pinch our skin and check our pulses and stare hard out into nothing. Dadi muttered prayers and rebraided my hair. Amil lay flat on his bedroll, staring at the sky. He held a smooth pebble in his hands, turning it over and over. Sometimes he would close his eyes, so I kept checking the pebble. He would stop for a few minutes, but then give it a turn or two and my heart would slow down. If I looked at Amil's empty face I would start crying, so I just watched the pebble in his hand. I had never seen him like this, so still and quiet.

I wasn't even thirsty anymore. I couldn't feel anything. The next thing I knew Papa was waking us up in the dark. The air had cooled. I looked out across the flat, dusty land and could see the slow glow of blue light over the horizon, the first sign of dawn. He had found more mangoes. When had he done this? He pulled off the skins.

"Eat," he said, handing them out to each of us. "You must. Suck out the juice."

We took the three slippery mangoes, taking weak bites, sucking on them like little babies. Papa had to hold Amil up with one hand and feed him the mango. Amil's eyes were unfocused. My throat tightened. I crawled over to him and held his cold, bony hand. If I lost my brother, I don't think I could ever utter a word again.

After we finished our mangoes, Papa squatted in front of our little circle facing us.

"Listen," he said in a hoarse whisper. "There is another village a mile from here. We need to go now. We have to use every bit of strength we have."

We nodded and hobbled up and somehow collected our things. I got a burning cramp in the calf of my leg and collapsed to the ground. I started getting them yesterday. I saw Amil and Dadi have them, too. For some reason Papa didn't have them or he hid it from us. He told us to flex our feet hard and rub the muscle to make them go away. As Papa helped Amil up, Amil bent over and vomited out his mango.

Dadi walked over and whispered something in Papa's ear. She shook her head. Papa nodded. They whispered some more, but I couldn't hear them. Papa helped Amil sit down again. My cramp faded as I rubbed.

"I don't think you can walk it. Rest here with Dadi," Papa said to me and Amil. "I will bring back water."

But what if we die before you come back? I wanted to ask. I didn't want to die, not like this. Is there any good way to die? Maybe when you're very old, surrounded by all who love you and your heart gently stops beating because you've had enough living. But we hadn't had enough. You didn't have enough either,

Mama. I knew I should be screaming and wailing. But I couldn't. I had nothing left in my body.

Papa looked hard at us and put his flat hand on my cheek. He checked Amil's pulse again and then I saw him take Amil's hand. He looked at Dadi.

"Keep talking to him. Try to get him to suck on a small amount of mango, not too much."

Then he took two water jugs and walked away from us toward the main path.

"Amil," I said, lying down next to him. "Let's count." He turned slightly toward me. "We'll count the number of footsteps it should take for Papa to walk a mile and back. It won't be long. He'll get us water."

I started counting softly. Amil watched me with his big dark eyes. Again, my mind flew backward to a night in our house long ago. Amil must have had a nightmare. He woke up shrieking. We were probably about seven. I got up and sat next to him. He lay back down and I held his hand. I told him to count as high as he could go. "Only think of the numbers and you won't think of anything else." We both counted, his eyes blinking at me. Eventually he went to sleep again. From then on, I did that with him whenever he had a nightmare. Now, here we were living in a nightmare.

Dadi crouched by Amil on his other side and fed him bits of mango. The mango I ate must have helped me, because the fog lifted a little bit. I counted up to one hundred, then two, then a thousand. I pictured Papa's steady steps marking the sandy path. Amil closed his eyes. His legs twitched. I watched his chest go up and down and matched my footstep counting with his slow breathing, counting three footsteps for every breath in and three more for every breath out. Dadi sat cross-legged and hummed softly, patting Amil's shoulder occasionally. I looked at her, my poor Dadi. Her tan and gold sari, tinged with dirt, her face dry and looking even more wrinkled. Her bun had fallen out and a long gray braid trailed down one shoulder. A burst of guilt burned in my cheeks thinking about how many times I'd wish she'd stop sucking her teeth or telling me to do my chores or braiding my hair too hard and too tight. She loved us. She was like an old, soft blanket that I barely even noticed was there. She just kept going, no matter what.

"Dadi," I said.

She looked up.

I tried to swallow, but my mouth muscles didn't quite work. "I love you."

She waved her hand at me and shook her head. She was right. I shouldn't be saying such a thing. But I needed to, in case. We never said those words to one another. But it didn't make me sad, because we did things that meant love. Now I could see it. Dadi washing and mending my clothes, Papa kissing us on our foreheads before bedtime, Amil making a drawing of me. Kazi making my favorite paratha stuffed with fried onions and potatoes. Every day had been filled with things like this. All love, even between Papa and Amil. Why hadn't I seen this before, Mama? What if it was too late? I reached out and took Dadi's dry, brown hand and squeezed. She squeezed mine back.

I didn't stop counting. I could think and count at the same time. Once in a while I'd lose my place a little bit. An hour had probably passed. I was on three thousand. I counted four steps now to every breath from Amil and then five. I shook him, but he didn't open his eyes.

"Amil," I whispered in his ear, and shook him again. Nothing.

"Dadi," I said, and looked at him. "He's not waking."

She shook his shoulder and pressed a piece of mango in his mouth, but he didn't stir. Her eyes flashed in panic. She pressed her head on his chest.

"He's breathing," she murmured, and then turned her head up to the sky. She began to wail out a prayer, not loud, just filled with pain. I wanted her to stop, but instead I looked up to see what she saw. And then I felt it—a spot of water on my head, tingling through to my scalp. I looked around me. I wondered if I was imagining it. Dadi kept wailing her prayer and I felt another drop. Dadi stopped and looked at me.

"Did you feel it?" she asked me.

I nodded. We both tipped our heads to the sky. More and more drops came down. I saw one land on Amil's forehead, though he didn't move.

The rain started to come down harder. I looked up and held my mouth open. A few drops fell in.

"Nisha, we need to collect the water!"

I started to feel dizzy as the water hit my arms, my face, inexplicably all this water. And yet it was still out of reach. I thought about the mortar and pestle I had hidden in my bag. I got it out and unwrapped it. I hadn't looked at it since we left. Just holding it in my hands felt like I had traveled back in time to our kitchen. Dadi watched me, surprise in her eyes, but she didn't say anything. I set the marble mortar down, the bottom of the little white bowl stained with crushed spices. It started to fill up. My throat ached. Then it was full enough for a drink. As much as every cell in my body longed for the few sips it contained, I crouched over Amil.

"Amil, wake up. I have water," I said, my voice sounding deep and scratchy, not my voice at all. He didn't stir. I slowly poured a bit in his mouth and rubbed his throat to help him swallow. He took in a dribble and then coughed. His eyes flicked open and he started to cough.

"Drink," I hissed in his ear as loud as I could in my dry voice. Dadi came and held his head up. I poured more water into his mouth. This time he took in a little more. Then I heard a voice from far away, floating out in the thick rain-filled air. When I tried to listen harder, I didn't hear it anymore. I focused on Amil again. His eyes had closed. I lifted my head to the sky and let the water fill my mouth and swallowed my first sip of water in two days, cool and so sweet. Liquid diamonds.

"Amil, Nisha," I heard. I squinted into the rain. I saw a figure, dark and wet carrying jugs.

"He's back," Dadi said.

My stomach flipped and my whole body cried out,

a sound that was more like the yelp of an animal than my own voice.

Papa's dark figure, blurred by sheets of rain, came into focus as he got closer. Then he was right there, standing in front of me and Dadi, who squatted by Amil. Papa fell to his knees on the other side of Amil, dropping the jugs. His face twisted up strangely in a way I'd never seen before. He crouched over and put his forehead on Amil's chest. Then he raised his head, covering his face. Was he crying? I had never seen Papa cry before. But when he lowered his hands, I saw he was laughing, rainwater streaming down his head and face, his arms now reaching toward the sky.

"Maybe the gods are listening," he said in a hoarse voice. He reached around all of our shoulders, pulling us close, our heads touching, covering Amil in a human tent. Papa loved us. I knew I would remember this forever, pack it away in my mind like I brought Kazi's mortar and pestle, and the dirt, and your jewelry, Mama.

I grabbed the jug and took a long pull on the water. It felt like breathing air after being suffocated. Papa pushed it away from my mouth. Was he angry with me? Was I being greedy?

"Go slow. You don't want to vomit it up."

I nodded, relieved. Dadi took some.

Papa turned back to Amil. He sat him up a little more against Dadi, took his pulse, and shook him hard.

"Wake, Amil," Papa said.

Amil's eyes opened and closed, but then he smiled a little.

Dadi and I looked at each other.

"Papa," Amil croaked, finally opening his eyes, and pulled on Papa's arm.

"Yes," Papa said gravely.

"Are we dead?" he said, smiling.

"You little devil," Papa said, and slapped him lightly with one hand while holding the jug for him to sip.

A joke. Amil made a joke. The joy was almost too much. I bent down and kissed him on his cheek. I think we might live, Mama. After we drank and rested for a while and drank some more in the rain, I started shivering and I looked at Amil. He was awake, but trembling. Dadi looked cold, too.

"We have to get to shelter," Papa said. "When I walked to the village up ahead, I saw a good place, an old hut. It's not far, maybe a half a mile."

Papa had found a handful of pistachios in the bottom of his bag, and we each had three. The pistachios exploded in my mouth with sweet, meaty flavor reminding me of how hungry I was.

We helped Amil stand up. Dadi and Papa each put one of his arms around them and pulled him along. They followed behind me. I didn't like being the leader of our caravan, but Papa said that was safer than me following behind. I had to carry two water jugs, Amil's bag, my bag, and both our bedrolls. I arranged them on my back, my body struggling against all the weight. Papa carried his stuff and Dadi's. We joined others on the path again, everyone wet and weighed down with rain. I looked at my feet, which were somehow managing to take one step after another and promised myself I wouldn't look at anything else until we arrived. We had to stop a few times for Amil to rest.

"I can't, Papa," Amil said on the third time he sank into the mud. He looked so helpless, water streaming down his head, his eyes wide and sunken. That anger in my belly came back. If Gandhiji was walking with us, could he tell me why we have all been sent into the wild like a bunch of starving goats? Maybe this is what those in charge really thought of us, India's people, when this decision was made. I ask myself again what this has to do with independence?

"You can," Papa told Amil in his calm doctor voice, which I had never heard him use on Amil and held out his hand for him. "Only a few minutes longer."

We waited and Amil once again rose slowly to his feet and put his arms around Papa and Dadi. We hobbled, soaked, on the path with many other families. Now there was too much water. How quickly things can change. Through the pelting rain, I could see the small buildings of the village up ahead. Papa said to turn toward the left. There was a broken-down wooden hut, but we couldn't see the entrance. When we got around to the other side, there were at least three other families packed into a single small room, seated on the ground. I guessed they were Muslim families from their clothing and from the topis the men were wearing. The door had been broken off. I stayed back with Dadi, and Papa brought Amil closer and peered inside.

I looked at Amil in front of me, hanging on Papa. His body trembled violently. Dadi's hand shook in mine, but not as bad as Amil's. I shivered a little, too, but still felt better than I did this morning. The air was warm even in the rain, but the water had soaked Amil to the bone. Papa went in front of me.

"We need shelter. My son will die if he doesn't get warm," Papa said to the people inside as plainly as if he were telling them the state of the weather. Nobody spoke. I could hear the rain pounding on the metal roof. One man raised his head and looked into Papa's eyes. Everyone watched the two men, their eyes locked. I thought about what happened on the trains. I thought about what Papa said about everyone killing everyone. Hindus, Muslims, Sikhs.

"I beg you. We are peaceful," Papa said, breaking the silence, his voice cracking. The man gave a slight nod and gestured with his chin to the side of the room. There was a shifting as they made room for us. I kept my eyes down.

We crouched by the wall and sat cross-legged on the ground. Amil sat in Papa's lap, and Papa put his arms around him as if he were little. Dadi and I sat in front of them. I was closest to the wall, and Dadi sat pressed against my wet arm. After a few minutes I started to feel the warmth of the bodies. I looked back slightly, but Amil still trembled. The minutes turned into hours and Amil stopped shivering.

The rain ended abruptly, and the sun started to burn through the clouds as if it hadn't just been pouring buckets a few minutes ago. My heart lifted and I rejoiced in the same sun that almost killed me. We all started to move out of the hut. Nobody spoke. The Muslim families gathered their things. We gathered ours. Papa put his hands together and nodded respectfully at the man. The man nodded back, then we went one way and they went the other.

As we walked, we took more long pulls of water, our heavy jugs refilled from the rain. Amil seemed a little steadier on his feet, and we joined the growing mass of people headed toward the border, still many miles away. I wondered what it would look like? Would there literally be a line, a wall, guards? I had never seen a border between countries before. The sun felt warm on my back, like a big hand. Go forward, Nisha, it said. It was you, Mama, wasn't it?

After a short while, we found another clump of brush and rock to set up camp. Many other families were doing the same. I wondered sometimes why we didn't talk to anyone. Normally groups this large would overflow with sounds—chatting, laughter, arguments, people calling one another's names, like the market on any given day. Were we changed forever now?

Papa said we should stop early today while the sun was still high, and he told us to spread out our things so they would dry. Amil rested on the ground, propped up against a narrow tree trunk. Dadi laid out our bedrolls and net. I went through my bag and unwrapped my diary with shaky, hungry hands. The shawl was wet, but the cover of the diary was only damp. A welcome relief spread through my chest, out to each arm and leg, to the tips of my fingers, even under my dirty fingernails. I put out the bag of jewelry and dirt and the mortar and pestle on the shawl with my diary on top of my extra salwar kameez and underwear. I didn't bother to hide anything anymore, and Papa didn't even give my things a second glance.

He started to collect dry sticks for a fire and I helped him. We only could find thin twigs under the brush which wouldn't burn very long, but we found many, and two thicker branches from the lower parts of a bush that seemed dry. He pulled the lentils and rice out from his bag and looked at Dadi.

"How much should I put in the pot?"

"Papa," I said before she could answer. "I'll do it."
I had watched Kazi cook lentils many times. Even
though we had no spices and we were cooking the lentils and rice together, which Kazi would never do at
home because it would make the rice mushy, I wanted
to watch the water boil. I needed to smell the sweet,
nutty steam.

Papa nodded, his lips turning up in a quick smile.
I took the damp bags from him and poured half lentils and half rice into the pot. My hands still shook,
but the empty pit of my stomach kept me going. I saw
Amil watching me. And then Dadi. They watched me
in silence like I was performing magic. I put in some
water just to cover it. I could add more if I needed
to. Papa had kept the matchbooks in his small leather
medicine bag, so they stayed dry. The scraps of wood,
still too damp, wouldn't light. We started hunting for
more twigs that had been under the trees and put
the damp ones out in the sun along with some dried
leaves. We would have to wait.

After some time, we tried again to light the fire. But
it was still too damp. I wanted to punch the ground
with my fists. I wanted to scream. I've never screamed,
at least since I can remember. Maybe I did when I

was a baby. I've heard Amil scream many times. He screamed for joy, running down the hill past the vegetable gardens. He screamed in anger when we fought. He even screamed at Papa when Papa told him he would take away all his drawing material if he didn't do better in school, and Papa swatted him in the face. Amil never did that again. I've always been afraid that if I screamed, I might break apart in a million pieces. But watching another match die out under the wet wood, I could feel the rush of energy in my throat. I could imagine myself screaming.

I stirred the pot which I had put down in the sun and took a spoonful of the uncooked lentils and rice in my mouth. It was like chewing on tiny pebbles. I passed it over to Dadi, who gave it to Amil, and then took a spoonful herself. Papa was fiddling with the stick pile and matches. The water had barely softened it. But still, it was so good to have something in my mouth. I kept biting down slowly and eventually swallowed it. I took another spoonful and then heard Papa yell out.

"I got it!" he said as small clouds of smoke drifted up into the air and a low flame started blooming on the mound of sticks and leaves. I hurried over with my pot and held it above the flame. The fire crackled and sputtered, but the flame stayed. We stared at the pot of rice and lentils like it was the most interesting thing we'd ever seen. After a few minutes, little bubbles sprouted up in the water. Dadi clapped her hands like a young girl. Papa said, "Aha!" and Amil managed a small whooping sound. I just held that pot as steady as I could over the center of the flame.

After twenty minutes the rice had swollen enough and absorbed some water. I stirred a bit more. The fire was now a decent size, and Papa kept adding small twigs that had sat in the sun. Finally, we kneeled, huddled together around the fire and passed around the pot, spooning lentils and rice in our mouths, soft and almost salty, big grins spreading over our faces. I would have never imagined it, all of us, shoulder to shoulder, warm and smiling. Papa put his arms around me and Amil again. The sun sank into the horizon and exploded in hot oranges and blues. I swallowed another mouthful and felt Papa's strong arm on my shoulders. Mama, it's so strange. At the end of the day we almost died, I was happier than I could ever remember.

Love, Nisha

August 25, 1947

Dear Mama,

We don't have much longer to go. We have jugs filled almost to the top and it didn't rain today. Papa said one more day and we will reach Rashid Uncle's house, your house, Mama. Did you and Rashid Uncle play together there like me and Amil? Did you climb trees and make pictures in the dirt with sticks and skip rocks in the rain puddles? I think Dadi said something about Rashid Uncle being your baby brother. If you were alive, you would be thirty-five. I wonder how old Rashid Uncle is, but I'm afraid to ask. I just know he's younger.

Our belongings dried in the sun. We were not attacked by any people or snakes or desert foxes or scorpions, so I think we're going to make it. I don't sleep well at night, though, and my head feels thick and dizzy. The ground is hard under my bedroll. I get sand in my ears and hair. I can hear the buzz of insects, the calling of a wildcat or wolf, and sometimes the voice of a person, a man or a woman calling out a name or yelling at their children. Sometimes I hear crying. We usually find a place tucked away far from others, though it's mostly sand and dirt as far as the eye can see. As our journey continues, there are more and more people going both ways. We all sleep close together right near the fire. Papa keeps it going most of the night, always on guard. Sometimes I wonder if he ever sleeps at all.

I got up early and started a small fire by myself. Papa had put a pile of twigs over the old fire the night before. I boiled some more rice and lentils, the smell waking me up and making me feel more normal. We have food for two more meals, but that should be enough. Already, I can feel my hip bones a little more when I lie down flat. It's only been a few days, but I was a little skinny to begin with, not as bad as Amil, but still too bony. At home, we always had enough to eat, but Papa doesn't like to have too much of anything, food, furniture, people. I remember looking at Sabeen, her rosy full cheeks and lips. Her mother, with her round belly and easy smile. I would feel jealous watching them together. They spent so much of their

time talking and laughing. Maybe someday, after all this, after we find a new life, a new home, with plenty of water and food, then I could grow up and have full rosy cheeks and a soft round belly. Maybe I could walk and talk and laugh with a daughter of my own.

The water will last us another two days if we're careful and nobody spills it. Papa has been so nice to Amil since he's been sick, but another spill could change that. When we're sick, we get the Papa everyone else gets, the calm, gentle doctor who makes you feel like it's going to be okay.

As I was stirring the pot of food while the sun came up, Amil tapped me on the shoulder. I jumped.

"Sorry," he whispered.

I smiled and shrugged. He had more color in his cheeks. I could tell even in the low light, and his eyes shone again. Amil was back.

"You were really sick," I whispered to him.

"I know," he said.

"I almost thought that—" But before I could say anything, he clamped his hand on my mouth.

"Shut up. Don't say it," he said.

He was right. I promised myself I would never speak of Amil almost dying again. I brushed his hand

away. "Your hand is disgusting," I said, feeling joy being able to tease my brother again.

"So is yours," he said, his eyes dancing around, a grin spreading across his face. He grabbed my hand that wasn't stirring and held it up to my eyes. I looked at my hand, the dirt creating little roads in the creases of my palms, like a map.

I pulled my hand back and took the pot off the fire. Papa sat up. Dadi was still sleeping. Usually Dadi was the first up. She probably needed some extra rest. How was she even okay? We passed the pot around, spooning in our warm breakfast, and again I couldn't believe how good the plain undercooked lentils and rice were. It was like I had a new tongue.

Dadi got up slowly and told us to have all the food.

"No, Ma, you have to eat," Papa said, and held a spoonful in front of her lips.

"We each had five spoonfuls," Amil said. "You have the rest, Dadi."

I was surprised he knew how much we each had. I wasn't counting. My stomach felt warm and not like a big, empty cave, but nowhere near full. I could have eaten two pots myself.

"You each have one more," she said quietly. "My

stomach today . . ." She touched it and turned her eyes to the ground.

"Ma," Papa said. "What do you mean?"

She waved his comment away. Papa held the spoon to her. She shook her head and her eyes hardened.

"Give it to them first," she said, looking at me and Amil. "I only want the last bite."

Papa hesitated. "Suresh," she said, and he did what he was told.

We packed up and joined the ever growing path of people going in two directions, with a big dip in the middle of paths set about fifty feet apart. I fell back into the pattern of my footsteps. I liked to listen to the rhythm. Dadi stood next to me, and Papa stood by Amil and we followed closely behind. Today Dadi was even slower.

"Are you okay, Dadi?" I asked her. I turned and saw my grandmother, her back looking a little more hunched in her dirty sari. Her gray hair fell out of her bun in pieces around her dull face. She glanced at me, her eyes not quite focusing on mine, and gave a little nod. I took her hand. She squeezed it and I squeezed back.

"Is Rashid Uncle nice?" I asked, surprising myself.

The words had started slipping from my mouth a little more easily. We were different here on this path, our hard cracked feet pounding the hard cracked earth. Nothing mattered here. Nothing was real. We didn't have neighbors. We didn't have a home. It was in-between living.

"Nice?" Dadi looked and blinked at me. She shook her head, not really saying yes or no. "We'll see, we'll see," she said, and squeezed my hand again.

Love, Nisha

August 26, 1947

Dear Mama,

Every night, except on the really bad day, I sit by the fire and write. The more I write, the clearer you get. I'm glad I brought three pencils. Papa helps me sharpen them with his knife, and he doesn't question me about my writing. He just lets me do it. I wonder what he would say if he knew I was writing to you.

Sometimes I hear you talking to me. You have a sweet, low voice. "Nisha, just one more step," you say. And I take it. You said to me when we were so thirsty, "Pretend the air is water. Drink it in." I did. Mama, I wouldn't ever say this to anyone else but if we died, would that mean we could be with you? But I'm not even sure if dying would mean that, so I keep going. I wouldn't hear your voice in my head if you didn't want me to keep going, right?

I see you now, walking with us, a red and gold scarf blowing behind you, just like the one I saw hanging in Papa's closet that he kept all these years, the one still in the closet waiting to be taken by strangers. You are the most beautiful person here on this dry, sad path. It's like we're all the color of dust and you are gold, and rich brown, in red and purple with dark-lined eyes and shiny red lips. You glow. I see the flash of your golden earrings. I hear the jingle of your bangles. You are here and I'm following you, Mama. You will take us to Rashid Uncle and you will take us to our new home.

Are you happy that we will be staying with Rashid

Uncle? I wonder if he is happy we are coming? Why didn't he ever try to see us? Is it because Papa told us we are Hindu and not both Muslim and Hindu after you died? Can you be both? Sometimes I don't really feel like anything, not Hindu, not Muslim. Is that a bad thing to feel? Papa told me Gandhiji believes we are everything anyway. I guess that makes the most sense to me. If everyone felt that way, we would have stayed in our home, a whole country, safe and truly free. I want to know what Rashid Uncle thinks of us, Mama. Tell me, soon, somehow.

Dadi is very tired now. She's lying by the fire, asleep before anyone. She drinks water, but eats no food. Amil asked Papa if she was sick, and I leaned in to hear the answer.

"She's old. This trip's too hard for her," Papa said in his way that isn't really answering anything. Then he turned and went back to shaking sand out of his bag. He's been checking her often, her pulse, her eyes, pinching her skin. She just waves him away, but she does not suck her teeth. She does not sing and she does not pray. There is so much silence I almost can't bare it. Amil doesn't even say much lately. I don't even hear much speaking from anyone walking around us. I need other voices. They fill me up. It's like we're all underwater, holding our breath until we can rise again into the air. Anything too loud, and we might all drown.

But I do hear the Azan, just like we heard every-day in Mirpur Khas when the Muslims stopped and prayed. Back in Mirpur Khas, I didn't think about it. It was part of the sounds of the day. The call would ring out from the village on loudspeakers at the mosque, and we could hear it trickle in through the windows. Kazi would stop what he was doing and get his prayer mat that he kept rolled up in the corner of the kitchen. He would wash, put the mat by the window, and stand, bend, kneel, touch his forehead to the ground, and stand again while he said his prayers.

We knew never to bother Kazi when he was pray-ing. Sometimes I thought of you, Mama. Did you pray five times a day? I've never seen Papa pray or sing. He says all we have is the here and now. I wonder if that's true. As we get closer to the border, I see more and more Muslims on the opposite path from India seeking new homes. Someone calls out the Azan and they stop and pray, and the people on our path keep moving. It makes me think of Kazi and I get sad, so

I don't look. I just walk, my eyes on the back of the person in front of me.

Today, though, you know what I did? When I heard the Azan, I said a prayer in my head. I made it up, combining what I've heard Kazi say and Dadi say. I don't know if it counted because I didn't know the exact words and I didn't kneel down, but I thought it couldn't hurt. I would never tell anyone this. They might be mad at me, mixing it all together and not being proper about it. But someone has to pray for Dadi. You would have prayed for her, right, Mama?

Love, Nisha

August 27, 1947

Dear Mama,

Papa told us tonight is the last night before we get to Rashid Uncle's. After we ate our mangoes, he handed us pieces of kaju katli. I turned the diamond-shaped candy over and over in my filthy hand. Why had he kept this from us? I wanted to throw it at him. What else was he holding on to? But my mouth watered at the thought of biting into it, enjoying the second of happiness it would give me. So I popped it into my mouth and held it there, letting it dissolve on my tongue. I watched Amil eat his. He had decided to nibble it like a tiny mouse. Our eyes met as we chewed. We didn't smile and we didn't speak. Was he thinking the same thing about Papa?

Our trip to Rashid Uncle is taking a day longer because Dadi needs to go slow. Papa, Amil, and I take turns helping her walk and she leans on us, her papery arm resting across our shoulders. Her bones feeling no heavier than a bird's. She finally ate some mango and has been drinking water, but she needs to rest often. We will get to Rashid Uncle's or we won't. Dadi will get better or she won't. We will get to our new home. Or we won't.

Love, Nisha

August 30, 1947

Dear Mama,

I'm sorry I couldn't write the last two nights, but now I can, lying here in an actual bed. Mama, why didn't Papa tell us about Rashid Uncle? It all makes more sense now and yet is only more confusing.

It was almost dusk when we finally walked close to where Papa said Rashid Uncle lived. He said we were several miles outside the city of Umerkot. We passed through a village and across some dusty farm-land. After several minutes in the low light I could see a cluster of homes, fairly large in size, all white. Papa turned to us and said, "This was the home your mother grew up in." Amil and I quickly looked at each other. Even though I had known it before, actually standing in front of your house was like having the wind knocked out of me. I could barely breathe. Papa said we should sit behind some bushes and wait until dark, then Papa would go see Rashid Uncle and make sure it was safe. He told us he didn't want anyone to see us go into the house.

"If a person comes up to you," he whispered, looking harshly at Amil, "tell them your grandmother needs to rest. Don't say more or less. But in the dark I don't think you'll be noticed. Many of these houses are empty now."

Amil nodded.

"When I whistle once," Papa continued, "then you come quietly and quickly and run right in that one," he pointed to a house in the middle of the cluster. "Don't talk and don't take off your packs. Be ready at any moment."

Amil and I glanced at each other.

"Understand?" Papa whispered.

"Yes, Papa," Amil and I whispered back.

We waited until nightfall and then Papa walked to the door. There was a full moon and a cloudless sky. The air smelled of burning wood. I could see Papa knock, and his tapping sound drifted out into the night followed by the whine of a hinge from the opening door. I could hear the murmur of voices and then the door close. We sat down holding our packs. Dadi lay against hers, propping her head up. I stared toward the direction of the door. A part of me hoped you'd be inside. Could you have been hiding there all along?

Amil started to play with the thin, frayed leather on

his sandals. I elbowed him and pointed through the bushes to keep him focused on the task. We waited and waited. I heard a rustling and my body froze, but when I turned nothing was there.

"Did you hear something?" I whispered to Amil.

"Yes," Amil said. We waited again, very still. The rustling grew.

"We need to move," Amil whispered. "Now."

We helped Dadi up and moved farther away from the bushes toward a dirt road we could see dimly outlined in the moonlight.

"We shouldn't go too far," whispered Dadi. We both held her by an arm helping her walk faster. The rustling had formed into footsteps, rushing closer and closer.

Someone grabbed my shoulder. I screamed. The sound burst painfully from me like blood. The person, a man, I could tell from the size of his hand, covered my mouth and held a knife up to my throat. The metal felt strangely smooth and warm. Dadi started crying.

"You killed my family," he spoke in my ear through gritted teeth.

I couldn't see him, only hear him, smell the scent of old sweat, and dirt, and sour breath. I could hear my breathing echoing in my ears. The side of the knife pressed harder. Dadi sank to the ground on her knees, her head bending toward our feet. I wasn't scared, only numb, and felt as if I was floating upward, toward the sky.

"Please, we didn't kill anyone," Amil kept yelling over and over, spit flying out of his mouth. Dadi was bending herself at his feet, praying. I stood absolutely still, trying to hold my neck back from the blade's edge. I wondered if I had stopped breathing, but somehow I kept on standing. The man's hands shook.

"My children, my wife. They're gone," he said, his voice breaking. "You killed them. You all killed them. They were only trying to get water and you killed them."

"No, sir, please. We are just walking to the border. My grandmother needed to rest. We didn't do anything to your family," Amil said as loud as he could. "We'll give you food, water, anything you want."

Then I heard the hinge and Papa's whistle.

We were all silent. He whistled again. The man pressed the flat side of the knife harder against my neck.

"I beg you. She's an innocent child," Dadi called out, her hands pressed together.

The man trembled, the knife shaking against me. "My family is dead and no one is innocent."

"My father and uncle are coming," Amil said, now in a lower tone. "They have guns."

I heard footsteps coming from the hut.

"Let her go," I heard Papa call in a voice so strong and mighty I wondered if it was even Papa.

"He has a gun," Amil said again, and I wished he really did.

The man's hands shook so much, he dropped his knife and let go of me. I broke away and ran toward Papa, holding my neck. Amil and Dadi clustered around Papa, too. There was no uncle.

"It doesn't matter if you shoot me. End my suffering, I beg you," the man said, and fell to his knees. I finally took a good look at him. He was a small man, his ankles no wider than Amil's. His hair was matted with dust and dirt. I could see dried blood on the sleeve of his kurta. "Hindus killed my family," he sobbed into his hands, his face pressed against them in the dirt. "Sliced their throats as I watched. And then I escaped, but I should have let them kill me, too." He wore a topi, so I knew he was Muslim, but how did he know we were Hindu? When we were in Mirpur Khas, it was easier to tell who was who, but out here, we all looked the same in our dirty clothes. Some of the Muslim men have lost their topis. Many people just drape whatever they can find over their heads to protect them from the sun. We grabbed on to Papa. I still felt so numb, not crying, not angry. It was so strange, Mama.

Papa shrugged us off gently and moved forward toward the man.

"Leave him alone," Dadi cried out. "He's dangerous." Papa didn't listen to Dadi and went over cautiously to the man. He picked up the man's knife and topi that had fallen off. He put his hand on his shoulder and held his belongings toward him. The man looked up, frightened.

"An eye for an eye makes the whole world blind," Papa said.

The man got up slowly and dusted himself off. He kept his head down as he took his topi and knife. Then he turned and ran off into the darkness. Papa had said those words before. They were Gandhiji's words. Now I knew what they meant. So a Hindu family kills a Muslim family, who kills a Hindu family, who kills a Muslim family. It would never end unless someone ended it. But who was going to do that?

We all moved forward, trying to see the path in the blue night. We stumbled a few times. Amil and Papa held Dadi up. I don't even know what kept me going. I remember walking through the doorway. As soon as I was inside the house, I couldn't see anymore, the tears, the horrible shaking, the fear all coming out. I couldn't breathe right and the room spun. Papa told me to put my head between my knees. That's all I remember.

Love, Nisha

August 31, 1947

Dear Mama,

When I woke up, I was lying on a bed, a real bed with a patterned blanket. I thought for a moment we were back in our house. Amil and Papa were hovering over me. It was strange to be inside. Then I remembered, this was your home, Mama! There was also a new person staring at me, standing by a doorway. I looked back at him. He wasn't too tall. He wore a topi on his head and a tan kurta. He dressed like Kazi. But his face was not like Kazi's at all. Something was wrong with it. He stood out of the light of the two candles burning on the table and I couldn't quite see, but his lip was raised up in the middle, exposing his gum and a few crooked teeth. His lip seemed like it was connected to the bottom of his nose.

Back in Mirpur Khas, a dried fruit vendor at the market had always worn a scarf over his mouth and nose, and Papa said it was because he had a cleft palate and showed me in his medical book what it was. Some people are born with it, Papa said, and most people could never afford the surgery to fix it. Sometimes hospitals helped if the person couldn't eat or swallow.

There was also a girl in my school, Mital. She didn't wear a scarf over her face. Her lip went up in the middle and touched her nose. She never spoke, like me. I don't know if it was because she couldn't or didn't want to. I suppose she could eat, because then she would have had the surgery. I never saw her doing so, though. I would try to look at her for more than a second, but I always turned away. I wanted to not care. I wanted to be her friend because she didn't have any. I only had Sabeen, who I wasn't even sure was a real friend because I never spoke to her. But it was too hard to look at Mital. I'm so ashamed when I think about it, which is why I usually don't. Did you have trouble looking at Rashid Uncle, Mama? Were you a coward, like me? I'm sure you were not.

"This is Rashid Uncle. He can't speak, only write," Papa said in his doctor voice. Rashid Uncle nodded at me. "Can you stand?" Papa asked.

I started to move. My neck hurt and it all flooded back to me, the memory like water filling an empty space. I remembered the man, his blade pressed to my neck, Amil yelling, Papa arriving just in time, and coming here. I stood and looked around the airy room with a colorful woven carpet on the floor and a carved chest of drawers that reminded me of my own, and I felt the sting of the memory. There was another bed on the opposite wall. Dadi lay there, asleep, her chest rising and falling slowly. I started to walk, my curiosity taking over, and Papa followed me. I stepped carefully into the hallway and past another open door. I looked in and saw a similar room, but smaller, with one bed along the window and another along the opposite wall. I peered into the third room. It had one large bed, a detailed tapestry hanging on the wall, a carpet, and a chest of drawers. I also saw an easel in the corner, with a blank canvas on it. I thought it must be Rashid Uncle's room.

I walked under an archway to a formal sitting room, with a long couch, several wooden chairs, embroidered pillows, and a low carved table in the middle. Paintings also hung on the walls. One was of a blue ocean against an even bluer sky in the first room. Another pictured a vase of flowers. I also saw a painting of a beautiful woman sitting cross-legged on the grass under a tree. It was you, Mama, I just know it.

In the dining room sat a table with six chairs and a heavy china cabinet with glass doors. A porcelain vase of pink and purple flowers stood in the center of the table, just like the painting. It was such a lovely place.

I turned thinking Papa was right behind me and found myself looking at Rashid Uncle's face. That's when I noticed his eyes. They look just like the picture of you, even more than Amil's do. Maybe there's a reason for all of this. I know this is a terrible thought, but if we never had to leave, we wouldn't have come here and had a chance to see Rashid Uncle's eyes, your eyes, alive. I quickly looked away.

"You can wash over there." Papa pointed toward a doorway in the back of the kitchen. I scrubbed my hands, face, and neck over the metal basin. I would need a full bath later to peel the layers of grime away, but it was so nice to see the skin on my hands not caked with dirt.

"How do you feel?" Papa asked after I was done.

"Okay," I said in a small, scratchy voice.

I saw one more painting in the kitchen. It was of Rashid Uncle himself, his face. I walked closer and studied the painting, his strange upturned mouth, like an invisible string pulled his top lip up from the middle, the shock of pink gum showing, the lopsided teeth one almost on top of another, his flat nose. It was easier to look at the picture, than the real Rashid Uncle. I can't believe he paints. Did you teach him or did he teach you?

"Nisha, come," Papa said sternly. I jumped, startled, and turned away from the painting. I followed him to the back of the house to check on Dadi, her pale face turned up to the ceiling, breathing weakly.

He bent down toward Dadi and touched her arm.

She opened her eyes and nodded. Then closed her eyes again. Papa headed to the kitchen. Amil had stayed with Dadi the entire time I walked through the house.

"Are you okay?" he asked.

"I think so," I said.

"I thought . . . I thought he was going to kill you," Amil said, his bottom lip trembling slightly. His eyes looked glassy.

"Papa was always going to come," I said, touching his hand and quickly shifted my gaze back to Dadi trying to be a little brave for Amil since he was so brave when we didn't have water. But I thought that he was going to kill me, too. The man could have easily slit my throat, and in a minute I would have been dead. There was nothing Papa could have done. There was something about having it happen that made me less scared instead of more scared. I don't know why. He was such a sad and frightened man. The way his hands shook. Why had his family been killed? Why would anyone do that? Do people who kill start out like me, or are they a different kind of human?

"It's strange that Rashid Uncle lives in this big house all alone. Did you see the paintings?"

Amil pumped his head up and down and grinned. "I guess that's why I can draw." Then his face grew serious again. "Do you think Dadi is going to die?"

"No," I whispered back harshly. "Can't you see she's just tired?" But I was thinking it, too.

"I'm going to ask Papa," Amil said, his eyes again bright and searching. I grabbed his arm, to stop him, but he slipped away from me and marched toward Papa and Rashid Uncle. I followed him down the long hallway, through the sitting room, and dining room, and into the kitchen. Papa stopped talking and they both looked at Amil. Amil gave Rashid Uncle one of his big, open smiles and my heart almost exploded. Amil has this way of smiling that makes you believe the world is a good place for at least that second. I feel differently about Amil now. I can't explain it. It's like he died and came back to life. I always liked his smile, but it makes me so happy now, like the first time I'm really seeing it. What would I do without Amil? He is my voice. He asks the questions I can't.

"Yes," Papa said.

Amil's smile disappeared. "Is Dadi going to die?"

Papa's eyes stayed on Amil. "I won't let her," he said, and then he left to check on her. But something about the stiff way Papa spoke made my stomach hurt. I reminded myself that Papa was a doctor. He had powers regular people didn't have. Did you think that about him, Mama? But then I thought about Amil. What saved Amil was really the rain, but it was Papa, too. Even if it hadn't rained, he still brought the water Amil needed. The way he stopped the man from hurting us and the way he was kind to him after. Papa might be the bravest person I know. But what Papa doesn't know is that Amil is almost as brave. I'm the coward. What did I do when the man attacked me? I froze. It was Amil who yelled and alerted Papa. It was Amil who said they had guns.

Rashid Uncle lit a fire in the enormous stove and boiled a pot of lentils. Then he chopped an onion. The smell tickled my nose. I moved a little closer. So did Amil. We watched as he fried the onion in a big pan and sprinkled in some mustard seed, garlic, salt, cumin, turmeric, and chopped ginger. He stirred the spices for another minute and poured in the boiled lentils.

"You don't have a cook?" Amil asked Uncle. I knew it was a rude question, but a big house needs a cook and a gardener and someone to tend to the housework. Rashid Uncle didn't do that all by himself, did he?

He looked up and shrugged, then went back to his stirring. Watching Rashid Uncle stir the steamy dal sent me spinning back to Kazi cooking in our kitchen; back to Dadi doing her normal caring for the house, rocking in her chair; back to Papa coming home from the hospital, kissing our foreheads good night. Back to me and Amil falling asleep with the taste of sweets on our tongues and thoughts of the things that happened at school that day. It had all been so ordinary, even boring, and now it seemed like a fairy tale. Tears started to fall. I couldn't help it. I put my face in my hands to cover them.

"Nish," Amil said. "What is it?"

I just shook my head.

"Rashid Uncle, can she stir?" Amil asked. Rashid Uncle stopped and turned. I forced myself not to look down, and he held out the spoon.

I blinked my tears away, stuck the spoon in the pot, and leaned over the warm yellow dal. I stirred so it wouldn't stick to the bottom. My body began to relax and I stirred some more. Amil knew me so well. All this time I thought he was just jumping around our house, trying to get out of chores and schoolwork just so he could play in the garden or draw. But now I see how closely he's watched me, how well he knows me, how much he has inside him. We stood there quietly for several minutes before Papa came over. I heard his footsteps stop and he watched me. After the dal was done, I put it aside.

Rashid Uncle opened up a pantry door and scooped some rice from a metal canister. He gave it to me and I poured in the right amount for five people. I watched his face. This time it was a little easier to look at him than it was minutes before. I stayed focused on his eyes. He took out a metal cup filled with water from a large jug to pour in the pot. He handed it to me and I poured. We put in four cups and waited for the water to boil. Kazi always boiled the water first before putting the rice in, but I didn't say anything. Rashid Uncle didn't seem like the most experienced cook. He chopped the onions every which way and didn't mince the ginger anywhere near as fine as Kazi would have. Maybe he had a cook who had to leave, a Hindu cook. My hunger started to make me dizzy. It hurt not to bring spoonful after spoonful into my mouth.

When it was done, Rashid Uncle took out five

bowls, and I spooned rice and dal into four of them and then one with just rice. He unwrapped four chapatis from a cloth and warmed them on the stove and stuck them on the sides of the bowls. I looked at the bowls, filled to the top with golden dal and rice, the toasted chapati sitting in the corner. It was the most food I had seen since we left home. I wondered if he always had such simple meals, but nothing had seemed so perfect to me.

"Take this to Dadi," Papa said to me, and handed me the plain bowl of rice. I nodded and swallowed the saliva collecting in my hungry mouth, cradling the warm bowl in my hands, and snuck a large pinch of rice. The sounds of chairs moving and the bowls being set down on the table startled me as I went into the other room. It was still strange to be inside, sitting at a proper dining room table for dinner.

Dadi had her eyes closed. I spoke her name and asked her to eat. Nothing happened. I put the rice under her nose and waited. After a few seconds, she opened her eyes and gave me a crooked nod. Then she waved me away. I looked in her face. It was drawn and dull.

"I will feed you," I said.

She stayed still, so I scooped a bit of rice into my

hand and pressed it to her lips. She took it and chewed. We did this a few more times. Then she put up her hand for me to stop.

"Good girl," she whispered. I put my hand over hers and held it there.

After a minute, I left the bowl of rice next to her and went into the other room. Amil, Papa, and Rashid Uncle had waited for me to eat. It must have been so hard for Amil and even Papa to do that. I sat down next to Amil and across from Papa. Then I ate. The rice, the dal, the chapatis exploded with flavor. I could taste the rich ghee, each grain of rice, each speck of cumin, the tang of ginger, garlic, onion. It was the best food I have ever eaten in my life.

No one spoke. After several large bites, I looked up at Papa and Amil, scooping up food with their chapatis fast and greedy. When we finished, there was enough for us to have seconds.

After the silent meal, Papa put his hand on Rashid Uncle's shoulder.

"I will never be able to repay the kindness you have shown us."

Rashid Uncle nodded and quickly started to clear the table.

We helped him clean the pots and dishes and then we were each able to shower. It took me a long time to get clean. I watched the brown water run down the drain and was afraid I'd use it all up. I didn't know I could ever get so dirty.

Amil and I asked to share the middle room. Papa slept in Dadi's to keep an eye on her. We got into bed and covered ourselves in our mosquito nets, feeling clean and new. Amil wondered if we could hide here until the fighting went away and then live here forever. I hoped so more than anything. If any new home made sense to me, this would be it. Then Kazi could come and live here eventually. Can I send that wish to you, Mama? Is this the bed you slept in? One more thing, please watch over Dadi. I can't lose her right now.

Love, Nisha

September 1, 1947

Dear Mama,

It is a new month and exactly seventeen days since the world changed. Is there another family living in our house yet? A happier family? Do they have more children with a mother and a father? I won't let myself think of our house burning to the ground or of Kazi sad and lonely. I try to think of everything alive, the garden colorful and bursting with vegetables, better than it was when we were there. I think of more children running around—four, two boys and two girls— a mother, calling them in for supper, checking to make sure their nails are clean, hugging them for no reason. I see a father coming home early, surprising everyone with rock candy sticks from the market, telling heroic stories from the hospital every night before bed. I think of the littlest girl finding Dee, my old doll, in the closet. It's the best surprise she ever got.

Love, Nisha

September 2, 1947

Dear Mama,

Papa says Rashid Uncle's house is a bit over halfway to the border. We still have many miles to go. When I ask Papa about when we're leaving, he says soon but he wants Dadi stronger before we do. I want to stay, but I'm also starting to feel trapped. We're not allowed to go outside. We are not supposed to be here, and I don't know what would happen if someone found out. Both Amil and I have heard Papa and Dadi talk about what they've read in the papers. I know lots of people have died walking and on the trains in both directions. The riots and killings keep happening. I still don't understand. We were all part of the same country last month, all these different people and religions living together. Now we are supposed to separate and hate one another. Does Papa secretly hate Rashid Uncle? Does Rashid Uncle secretly hate us? Where do

Amil and I fit in to all of this hate? Can you hate half of a person?

Rashid Uncle moves around the house so quietly. I worry that he's angry and wishes we weren't here. He gets food for us at the market and brings water from the well. I heard Papa ask him to go to two different markets so it won't look like more people are staying here. He nodded. Then Papa tried to give him money but he wouldn't take it. I hope that means he wants to help us.

Amil and I play guessing games and make up little stories and dances to keep ourselves busy. In the stories I always start with a girl or a boy, and he or she is running from something like a man with a gun or a knife or a big fiery torch. I say something bad that happens to the character and Amil says something good. Then I say something bad. Or we do it the opposite way. At the end the character always dies. We try to make the death worse every time. The worse the death, the funnier we find the story. We try to laugh quietly which makes it even funnier. We would have never made up stories like this before, and we would have never found them funny. Amil says it's because nothing's real right now. I know what he means.

Meals are my favorite time because I help Rashid Uncle cook. I just started doing it that first night and no one has told me to stop. We make simple things, dal, rice, spinach cooked with tomatoes, chapatis. I do most of it. I still wonder if Uncle always ate in this simple way. He makes sure I have the right bowls or the proper amount of rice but seems happy for me to cook. I make the same things I watched Kazi cook all my life. But cooking with Rashid Uncle is nothing like cooking with Kazi. He doesn't look at me and he can't talk to me, so it's silent. I want to ask him so many questions about you, Mama, but I'm too afraid. Not being able to ask him questions pains me in a new way. It's like I'm sick with all the words I hold on to and can't say. When Papa talks to Uncle, he writes back quickly and doesn't seem annoyed. Amil and Dadi talk to him, too, sometimes.

I noticed there was something familiar about Rashid Uncle, his movements, his bent head, the way he holds his shoulders. But I couldn't place it. Then I noticed the way he took a bowl from the table and circled it carefully with his long fingers. It reminded me of myself. So maybe he's like you, Mama, which means you and I are alike. I want to tell him this, yet I can't. I've looked through the house, to try and find some signs of you, maybe a piece of jewelry or a scarf, but I don't even know what I'm looking for.

How did I get to be this way? I'm just like Rashid Uncle, born with a defect that makes it hard to speak, even impossible, except that you can't see mine. Or maybe it's my fault. I'm just not strong enough. If we leave here, I may never see Rashid Uncle again. It is my only chance to find out more about you and I can't even say one word to him. Amil talks to Rashid Uncle, but Rashid Uncle only nods or writes down a word or two. He seems more comfortable with Papa, but maybe Amil won't mind asking some questions for me.

I wish we could go outside and play, then my mind wouldn't have so much time to think about the bad things. The good thing is that Dadi seems to have gained some strength from the food and rest. She still sleeps a lot, but spends time awake praying and singing her songs softly. She's eating more. She stayed up with Papa tonight after dinner in the sitting room. Amil and I lay on the couch, and I read him the scorpion section in the encyclopedia. Rashid Uncle sat at the dining room table and carved some wood. It made me feel like we've all lived here in this house our whole lives and nothing was wrong at all.

When Rashid Uncle comes home after working at his furniture business and going to the market, he sits at the table and carves. He's working on a small bowl and a horse. I secretly watch him. Maybe Uncle will teach us how to carve. He seems to have magical fingers. He makes all the ridges and bumps look so smooth, like they were never even there.

Love, Nisha

September 3, 1947

Dear Mama,

Today I saw something. It was a normal thing to see, but to me I thought I might be dreaming. That's what Amil means about things not feeling real. A regular person can seem like a vision.

I was looking out the window. There is a house maybe a hundred feet away. Our bedroom window looks toward the other house's back patio and garden. I was watching a dry leaf swirl and twist in the wind and she suddenly appeared. Why hadn't I noticed her before? I closed my eyes for a second wondering if she would be there when I opened them. She remained, even clearer than before, with a glistening black braid down her back, simply playing, not running or hiding, just being. I turned quickly to tell Amil and saw him drawing on some newspaper advertisements that Dadi gave him. He sat on the floor, cross-legged, his back to me hunched over his work, and I decided to keep watching without saying a word.

The girl lay sticks on the ground in circles. Then she stood and tossed pebbles into them. I squinted and watched her more. She spun around, smiled, and moved her mouth like she was talking to herself until she was called in, probably by her mother. It was hard to tell, but she looked about my age, maybe a little younger. Does she not have any siblings? I never knew anyone who didn't and I wonder if something bad happened to them.

As I watched her play, I felt the urge to climb out

the window and join her. The desire felt so strong I had to grip the windowsill to keep me in my place. She disappeared as quickly as she appeared. If I were allowed to play with her, I would talk to her, I promise, Mama. I wouldn't waste it. It's like the rules are different now. I wonder what would happen if she saw me?

Love, Nisha

September 4, 1947

Dear Mama,

I didn't see the girl today. I probably imagined her or maybe I just dreamed of her and my memory is all mixed up, but I couldn't stop thinking about it. Rashid Uncle stayed out most of the day, then carved wood outside under a tree. I really want to be friendly with him so I can find out more about you, but he doesn't seem to want to be with us. All Papa and Dadi do is read the papers, discuss things in whispers, and drink cup after cup of watery tea. Rashid Uncle brings back food which is the most exciting part of the day. I try to read the papers, but Papa and Dadi don't let us.

I manage to sneak looks at the headlines. Sometimes I see a string of words: *India-Pakistan Officials Discuss New Potential Violence* or *Communal Strife Continues* or *Gandhi Fasts for Peace*. Then they shoo me away. Papa did talk a little about Gandhi's fast. He told us Gandhiji said he wouldn't eat until people stopped fighting. Maybe it will work. Maybe tomorrow will be the day we taste true freedom. At night they take the papers to bed with them and hide them under their mattresses or have Rashid Uncle put them outside. Why don't they want me to see what I already know now—that the world is broken.

Love, Nisha

September 5, 1947

Dear Mama,

I did something today, Mama. I'm not sure why I did it after everything that happened with the man and his knife. I know now that this new world is dangerous, but are Amil and I just supposed to live here inside like prisoners? I'm so sorry, Mama. Your house is lovely, but lately I feel so angry and I don't know why or exactly at who. What would Gandhiji say? Would he be disappointed in me? Papa would. I just want to be free. Wasn't independence from the British supposed to free us? We've never been less free.

The girl came back when Amil, Papa, and Dadi were in the dining room. Papa now lets Amil sit at the table and draw. Papa knows Amil is not going to try to read over his shoulder. I didn't mind being alone. I wanted to watch out the window in case I wasn't dreaming. She didn't come out all morning, but then after lunch she was there, as if she had been there all along. When I saw her, I felt like someone threw cold water on my face. I'm not imagining things. She is real.

She sat on the ground braiding and unbraiding her hair, biting her lip with a scowl. Each time she did it, she shook her head and started to undo it. After a while she looked up. I raised my head fully over the window ledge. I waited for her to look in my direction. Papa, Dadi, and Amil seemed quiet enough. She turned toward me, and I stuck my hand out the window and waved. She seemed to raise her hand as if to wave back, but then she lowered it and quickly ran inside. My heart beat so fast I thought my chest was going to explode. What if she told her family I was there? Would we be in danger? Would people come after us like the man in the woods did? I spent the rest of the day sitting in the corner staring at my feet. I was probably too far away for her to see me, I tried to tell myself. I was afraid if I moved something terrible would happen.

"What's wrong, Nisha?" Amil asked me.

"Nothing," I said.

"But something is," Amil said. "I can tell."

"I'm just sad," I told him.

He nodded, looking carefully at my face. "You don't look sad, you look scared," he finally said.

"Just go away," I murmured. Sometimes I hated that Amil knew me so well. I didn't dare look out the window again and nothing happened.

Love, Nisha

September 6, 1947

Dear Mama,

This morning I decided to just peek out the window for a second and there she was. Nobody came to talk to us, or hurt us since I waved yesterday. Amil sat on his bed drawing pictures in the air, humming softly to himself. I was glad he wasn't paying attention. She sat on the ground. I couldn't see exactly what she was doing. I lifted up the window and leaned out a bit. It looked like she was weaving necklaces and bracelets out of weeds. That was something I always liked to do outside. I remembered the party when we left, weaving necklaces with my cousins. Could it really be so wrong if I played with her?

After she finished, her head turned toward me again. I moved closer to the center of the open window, and she looked me dead in the eye. After a few seconds, I waved again, holding my breath. This time she waved quickly before running back inside. A tingly feeling ran through my body, like I had opened a gift covered in shiny English wrapping paper and bows.

"What are you waving at?" Amil asked me, looking up from the floor.

"Nothing," I said.

He got up and looked outside. Then he looked back at me.

"Did you see someone out there?"

I didn't answer. He watched me, hands on his bony hips, squinting harder and harder. We stood there for a minute in a staring war. My nose started to twitch. I broke my gaze.

"It was a girl who lives in the house next door," I said, pointing toward it. "But she's gone now." I turned my eyes toward the floor, the words falling out of my mouth. "She waved at me."

I raised my head and watched his eyes grow wide. Then he smiled.

"Brilliant," he said in English.

I started to laugh and I couldn't stop. Amil joined me. We laughed until tears began to run down our faces. After a minute, I wasn't sure if I was laughing or crying. Once Papa brought home a British doctor who was visiting the hospital. After dinner, he and Papa smoked cigars in the living room and spoke in English while Amil and I secretly crouched by the door of our room and spied on them, trying to figure out what they were saying. We only knew a bit of English. The man kept saying the word "brilliant" after Papa spoke. The word seemed to please Papa and made his eyes sparkle. Amil and I figured it must mean something wonderful to make Papa look so happy. Sometimes we say it to each other when no one else is listening. It's the funniest word. It feels like feathers in my mouth.

I couldn't keep the girl a secret from Amil. If Amil doesn't know about it, it's like it's not really happening. And I want it to be real, Mama.

Love, Nisha

September 7, 1947

Dear Mama,

We waited for her together this morning when Dadi and Papa became absorbed in their reading. The girl came out but didn't look toward us. She didn't really do much of anything, just walked around in circles and occasionally squatted down and examined something on the ground.

"Let's give her a note somehow, ask her to come over to the window," I whispered to him.

He looked at me in surprise, his eyes twinkling with mischief.

"What if she tells on us?" he asked as we looked at her as she now sat cross-legged on the ground, scraping the dirt with a rock.

I told him she wouldn't. I believed that she would have already told on me if she wanted to.

"We could tell her we'll all be killed if she does," he said plainly.

My mouth hung open. Would we? Maybe it was too dangerous. We should just leave her alone, but then I felt a growing rage deep in my chest. It was okay for a strange man to put a knife at my throat, but it wasn't okay for us to speak to a little girl playing in the back of her house? I put my hands on Amil's shoulders. "Everything is dangerous now anyway. All we want to do is talk to a girl. It'll be okay."

Amil thought about it. "Let's check and see what Papa and Dadi are doing."

We headed down the hallway, through the sitting room, and into the dining room, where Dadi and Papa looked up from the table. "Why are you two sneaking about?" Papa said in a low, hoarse tone.

"We're just playing around," Amil said.

"Playing around?" Dadi asked. I shrugged and Amil ignored her. Her color was back. That made me feel better. I sat down next to her. She patted my shoulder and folded the paper. Amil started pacing around the table, skipping a bit. Amil used to spend hours running around the gardens, playing with friends, skipping and hopping to and from school. It was awful to say, but in some ways walking in the desert, at least when we still had water, might have been easier for him than being cooped up like this.

Just as Papa looked up at Amil, the annoyance flickering in his eyes, I heard something. It was a faint sound, but not a bird. I listened closer and I realized it was a song being sung by a child. By the girl. We all raised our heads and listened. It was the sweetest sound I had heard in so long. I think Papa, Dadi, and Amil thought so, too, because we all remained quiet and still until she stopped. But I was afraid somehow they'd know what we were about to do, that they'd want to look out the window toward the sound. The girl might see them and somehow that would be much worse than her just seeing us.

After a few minutes, the song ended and Papa and Dadi started reading again, as if nothing had happened. I wondered why they did this, but maybe they were afraid of our questions. Amil drifted away to our room and I followed him. We watched her again. Now, she was digging a hole with a stick.

Amil held out the torn edge of a newspaper in his palm.

"Where did you get that?"

"From the pages Dadi gave me. We can wrap it around a little rock and throw it near her."

"It wouldn't go that far," I said. Then I imagined her coming over. We could talk to her out the window in whispers. We could find out things. Maybe she was as lonely as we were.

I told Amil to get me a pencil after a few seconds. He quickly got one from his bag. I thought for a moment and wrote *Come to our window. We want to meet you. But don't tell anyone or bad things could happen.*

Amil nodded. Would Rashid Uncle's neighbors even be mad that we were here? What if Uncle was friends with them? Maybe they even knew we were here. I wondered again what the rules were exactly.

"Guard me," Amil said, grabbing the note and starting to climb out the window.

"Wait," I hissed at him. "You're going outside?"

He stopped. "How else am I going to get her the note?"

I pushed my head out the window and looked around. I couldn't see anyone else. Before I could say anything, Amil lifted both legs over the sill and suddenly he was standing on the ground outside. My heart pounded so hard my face throbbed. He picked up a small rock and wrapped the note tightly around it, walked a few feet closer, and threw the rock toward the girl. She quickly glanced at it when it landed and then looked up toward the direction it came from, startled. Amil scrambled back inside. We ducked under the window for a few seconds until we got the courage to peek over the ledge. We watched her as she slowly walked over to the rock and picked it up. She squinted in the direction of our window, unwrapped the paper, and read our words. She gazed out again toward us and narrowed her eyes. We poked our heads up farther.

"We've done it now," Amil said.

I nodded. The girl looked around and slowly walked in our direction. We held our breath as she came closer and closer. She stepped over the low stone border and onto Uncle's property. When she stood about ten feet away, I could see she was younger than I had thought. Maybe only nine. Amil put his finger over his mouth.

"Whisper," he said.

She nodded and came closer. "Who are you?" she asked. "Where did the man with the broken face go?"

Amil looked at me with questioning eyes. He didn't

know what to say. I opened my mouth, but I felt like I would faint. I closed it. I shook my head.

"She doesn't like to talk," he said, pointing to me. "We're from Mirpur Khas."

"Are you staying here for a long time?" she asked.

"No," Amil said. "We're on our way to the border."

"Oh," she said, and her eyes widened with under-standing. "So are you hiding here?" she asked, her face growing worried.

I swallowed.

"That's why you can't tell anyone we're talking to you," Amil said.

She looked around quickly in fear and started to back away.

"Don't go," I said in a whisper, and reached out as if to grab her hand, but she wasn't close enough. "Nobody is going to do anything if they don't catch us," I said, my voice a little bit louder.

Amil gaped at me, his mouth hanging open.

I shot him a mean look. The girl looked back and forth at us, still deciding if she wanted to stay.

"What's your name?" I asked.

"Hafa," she said shyly.

"I'm Nisha. This is Amil," I said.

Then Amil elbowed me in the ribs. "I think I heard a chair move," he said.

I looked back and listened.

"We have to go. Come visit us tomorrow in secret. Tell no one," I said in my most serious voice.

She nodded and skipped away toward her house.

I heard the creaky front door open and close. That meant Rashid Uncle was home.

"Do you think Uncle noticed anything?" Amil whispered in my ear.

"I don't think you can see the back of the houses from the path. But I'm not sure," I said, again my pulse racing. But, Mama, can I tell you something? I felt so happy, I didn't care.

"You talked to her," Amil said. I just nodded, bits of joy sparking through my limbs.

"Nisha, Amil, come help for dinner," Papa called from the other room.

We went and watched Rashid Uncle unpack the food. There were several sweet potatoes, green beans, two onions, and two cucumbers. He never got meat, though I was craving chicken or mutton. I don't know if he didn't eat it or thought we didn't. Maybe it was too expensive. My mouth watered at the thought of eating sweet potato, though. I couldn't remember the last time I had one. I didn't know any recipes that Kazi made with them, but we could fry them with the onions and the beans. I could taste it, sweet, salty, and spicy all together.

I got to work, rolling up my sleeves and clearing a space for chopping. Rashid Uncle handed me a knife.

After talking to Hafa, I felt different, like maybe I could be a new person. "Thank you," I said.

Rashid Uncle looked at me, surprised, and I met his eyes. He nodded and his mouth twitched. Then he started to measure the rice. We cooked quietly and afterward I spooned the fried vegetables and rice in bowls.

"Wonderful," Papa said, taking in the bright orange cubes of sweet potato nestled among the fried green beans and onions. Then he patted his stomach. We all ate slowly, savoring it. Amil normally shoveled his food in so fast, I wondered how he tasted anything, but even he seemed to slow down and enjoy it. We cleared our plates and Amil and I washed everything.

Papa and Dadi were having their last cup of tea for the night and Rashid Uncle sat at the table carving like he usually did.

I took in a deep breath. Amil watched me.

"What are you making?" I asked Rashid Uncle. Then I handed him his little chalkboard that he wrote on.

Dadi and Papa both put their papers down and looked at us. Rashid Uncle stopped and lowered his tool and small piece of wood. He had just started. It didn't look like anything yet. He took the chalkboard and a piece of chalk, moving slowly, carefully. *A doll*, he wrote. I thought of my old doll, Dee, and my stomach clenched. I nodded, but then my mouth went dry and I knew the words were stuck. My face grew hot. I shook my head.

Rashid Uncle looked at me carefully, studying my face.

*You have your mother's mouth*, he wrote. I looked at Papa and Dadi. They seemed frozen. Amil moved closer to me.

*And you, your mother's eyes*, he wrote and held it up toward Amil. Amil touched the corner of his eye.

*It makes me so happy to see your faces*, he continued.

He knew her. He could see her in our faces. It was like another universe had opened.

"Did you, was she," Amil stuttered. "Was she good to you?" he asked.

Rashid Uncle nodded.

*She loved you both before you were born,* he wrote.

I heard a little moan from Dadi, like she was crying. I heard Papa clear his throat. My body felt like it was melting. "Thank you," I whispered. It was the answer I had always wanted to hear. It almost made everything we had been through worth it. The tearing of India. The tearing of walls. Then opening of something new, of this. You loved us, Mama.

Love, Nisha

September 8, 1947

Dear Mama,

I woke up early this morning. Amil was still asleep. Amil looked like a very young child when he slept, and it made me want to touch his cheek. Sometimes when Amil slept too long in the mornings at home, I used to poke his cheek so I could watch his puffy eyes open for the first time that day. He would start to move and rub his eyes with curled fists, gazing at me like a much younger child. He was never mad at me for waking him.

I went into the kitchen and saw Rashid Uncle tinkering around, lighting the stove and warming a pot of water for tea. He noticed me and his mouth stretched wider. It's the way I know he's smiling. Papa already sat at the dining room table reading yesterday's newspaper. Dadi remained asleep.

"Good morning," I said shyly, and Rashid Uncle gave me a nod of his head in reply. After the tea was done, he started to heat the oil for poori just like Kazi used to do every morning at home. He gave me a cup of milk, and I sat down to drink it. Then he handed me the bowl of flour. I got up and poured some water in the flour and mixed the dough quickly, forming it into little balls, then flattening them into circles. I handed them to Rashid Uncle, who fried them in the hot oil. I watched each circle puff up and felt a lightness I hadn't felt in so long. We sat down and ate them warm with dal. I liked cracking the middle of the poori and filling it with dal, and taking a big, messy bite, smooth and crispy all at once. After breakfast, Rashid Uncle tapped me on the shoulder. I jumped a little, surprised. He held up the chalkboard. *The doll I'm making is for you,* it said. Then he pointed to a small block of roughly carved wood sitting on top of the stool he sat on to do his work. I could see the rough shape of a head and shoulders. I was too old for dolls, but I would never tell Rashid Uncle that. I went over and touched the wood, feeling the bumpiness of it. He hadn't smoothed out all the edges yet.

"Thank you," I said, bowing my head a little. "I will keep it always."

Something has changed. I'm starting to feel happy here. I'm starting to feel like it's home. We survived the walking, the thirst, the tiredness, the hunger, the man with a knife. Rashid Uncle told us you loved us. I talked to him. I spoke to Hafa. It has made me feel strong, Mama, strong and brave. Now more than ever I hope if we stay long enough, hide long enough, everyone will forget how mad they are and Hafa and I will be friends, real friends. Rashid Uncle will be my real uncle.

Later, Amil and I waited for Papa and Dadi to

start reading and Rashid Uncle to go out before we watched by the window. We sang loudly and told stories so Papa and Dadi would think that's all we were doing. Hafa didn't come for a while. We started to think that we had scared her off and both slid down below the window, our backs against the wall, staring out in front of us. I looked at our bags and bedrolls neatly stored in the corner. Papa made us pack up every morning and Amil would ask if we were leaving. Papa would shake his head.

"But when?" Amil would say, like he really wanted to leave. I know he hates feeling trapped inside, but did he forget that we almost died out there?

"The longer we stay out of harm's way the better," Papa said. "Be thankful we're here."

"Then why do we have to pack up every day?" Amil would say, but Papa never answered.

Maybe Papa wants to stay forever, too. I stayed quiet, looking down. All I could think of was talking to Hafa again. We waited until we saw her. She came out and acted like she didn't notice us. We watched her draw in the dirt, sing, run, cartwheel. She took out her messy braid and rebraided it again. Then she finally turned and squinted toward us. Amil waved a hand outside. She kept squinting and went back to her hair. Why wasn't she coming over? Didn't she want to be my friend as much as I wanted to be hers?

She looked around and started walking over and came up to the window. I'll try to remember everything she said, Mama.

"I know you were watching me, but I was too scared. Now my father is out and my mother is sewing in the back room," she told us. "She's not near the window."

"Why don't you have any brothers or sisters?" Amil asked. I glared at him. Wasn't this impolite? But then I turned to Hafa. I wanted to know, too.

"I do," she said. "Two brothers. They're a lot older."

Then we eyed each other in silence. I thought I heard a chair scrape the floor. We stopped, but heard nothing more.

"Where are they?" I asked softly. I still couldn't speak without my heart pounding in my ears.

Hafa kicked at the dirt with one foot. She raised her head, her eyes sad.

"We don't know. They left when the men came with fire to get all the Hindus and Sikhs out of the village. My brothers went with them, to fight for Pakistan."

We were all quiet again. Then Amil spoke.

"So you're not supposed to like us," Amil said.

I sucked in my breath. Why was he saying this? I wanted to clamp my hand over his mouth, drag him away. Papa told him not to speak about these things.

"And you're not supposed to like me because I'm Muslim," Hafa said.

"But it's so strange," I said. I couldn't explain the aching I felt deep in my stomach when I watched her, like all I had ever wanted to do was be friends with this girl.

"All my friends left the village. They were Hindu and Sikh," she said, glancing down again.

We were quiet. I knew what I wanted to say. I practiced in my head. Four words. Just four words. The blood flowed. There was a pounding in my chest, in my ears. I cleared my throat, licked my lips. I opened my mouth, and closed it again. Then I opened it and pushed out the words.

"My mother was Muslim," I said. "The man who lives here is our uncle."

Amil stared at me.

"Oh," Hafa said, a little smile sneaking onto her face.

"Yes," Amil said. "That means we belong on both sides."

"You're lucky," Hafa said.

"I guess so," Amil said. "It doesn't feel that way."

"Does that mean you're staying here?" Hafa asked, standing on her toes for a second and lowering her feet again.

"I wish we could," I said.

Amil looked at me and shook his head. "But we can't."

"Why?" Hafa asked.

"Because our mother is dead," Amil said, "and as far as other people know, we're only Hindu and have to go."

"Oh," Hafa said. "That's sad, about your mother."

"It is," Amil said. I nodded.

"Can I come inside for a minute?" asked Hafa. "I'll just climb in the window. My mother won't notice right now. She doesn't notice anything else when she's doing her sewing."

Amil and I looked at each other. If we heard Papa or Dadi walking down the hallway, we'd have enough time to get Hafa out. Amil closed our bedroom door quietly.

"They're just reading," Amil said. "They won't suspect anything."

Hafa hopped easily through the open window.

My breathing immediately quickened. "I don't know," I said in a shaky voice.

"We'll have a signal," Amil said. "If anyone hears a chair move or footsteps or a voice, they should put their hand on their head and Hafa will jump out the window."

Hafa and I nodded gravely. Hafa's long braid, longer than mine, had started to come loose and she didn't have a tie. Thick pieces fell around her face. She reached her hands backward trying to collect it all.

"Can you help me?" she asked, her eyes bright and clear.

"Me?" I asked pointing to myself, jolted upright with surprise.

"Do you know how to braid hair? I can't do it well on my own head. My mother didn't do it tight enough today, and we couldn't find the tie. I won't put twine in my hair, only my green ribbon, but it's lost." Her smile turned to a frown.

"Okay," I said a little too loud. She turned around and I carefully gathered her hair into my hands. Dadi taught me how when I was little. Her hair felt soft and smooth, not coarse and wavy like mine. I sectioned it into three bunches. Amil watched us in silence. Then I slowly wove each outside section in between the other as tightly as I could.

"Let me know if I'm hurting you," I said.

"No, that's good. Make it tight."

As I finished the last weave, she turned around.

"How does it look?" she asked.

I studied her face, her hair pulled back neatly now. Thick eyebrows framed her dark eyes and her small mouth curved up into a smile.

"Beautiful," I said. She laughed and touched the braid.

"Want me to do yours?" she asked, and I let her. She moved through my hair slowly, undoing the knots as she went. My face colored.

"I don't have a brush since we—"

"It's okay," she spoke over my words. "It'll look nice this way."

She finished and admired her work. "Much better."

I smiled shyly.

"I hear them," Amil whispered, putting his hand on his head. Hafa scrambled out the window before we could say anything else. Dadi opened the door and eyed us.

"Were you talking to someone?" she asked.

"Who would we be talking to besides each other?" Amil said quickly.

"I don't know," Dadi said, still squinting at us.

"You braided your hair," Dadi said.

I touched my braid and nodded.

"I helped her," Amil said, puffing up his chest. I gave him a quick sideways glance. Why did he have to say that? Dadi would know he was lying.

"I see," she said, and slowly shuffled away.

Once she was gone, Amil and I sunk to the ground.

"Don't ruin it," I whispered.

"Well, then you talk. Don't leave it all to me. You don't seem to have trouble talking to Hafa."

I shrugged and leaned my head back against the wall. A smile crept onto my face. Why didn't I have trouble talking to Hafa? I could still feel the silkiness of her hair in my hands. Maybe if Papa finds out and her parents find out, they will see that we're just two lonely girls who want to be friends. How could a friendship be dangerous?

Love, Nisha

September 9, 1947

Dear Mama,

Hafa came again today.

"I brought you something," Hafa said at the window.

Amil and I stuck our heads out.

"Give me your hand," she said, looking my way.

"Me?" I asked pointing to myself. When had another girl ever given me anything? I stuck my hand out slowly.

She thrust a bit of thin red ribbon into it.

"My mother brought me a new one, but it was too long, so I cut it in half." She turned and showed me the tiny ribbon at the end of her tight shiny braid. Her mother must have done it for her. "And you can have the other piece."

I closed my hand around it and felt like I was going to cry.

"Thank you," I managed to say.

"Why do you look so sad?" she asked.

"Oh, I'm not," I said. "I'm very happy."

"I'm so glad you're both here," she said, looking at

Amil now. "I was so lonely. Please stay?" she asked.

"Sometimes things can happen like that," Amil said. "Grown-ups just do things and no one knows why."

I nodded and so did Hafa. Maybe we could ask Papa. People do stop fighting, eventually, don't they? Amil asked if he could see my ribbon, but then we heard the scrape of a chair and Amil whispered "go," to Hafa and off she ran. I wanted her to braid my hair and tie it with the ribbon, but then Dadi would ask me where I got it. Papa probably wouldn't notice, though. It was a false alarm. No one came to check on us, but Hafa didn't come back today. I clutched the ribbon in my sweaty hand for a long time, then put it in the little pouch with your jewelry. I won't be able to wear it here. I hope that doesn't hurt Hafa's feelings. I'll explain it to her tomorrow. Mama, I have a real friend who I can talk to. Can you believe it?

Love, Nisha

September 10, 1947

Dear Mama,

The next day, we popped our heads out the window and waited a long time. As we waited, a panic started to take hold of me. What if I never saw her again? Finally, Hafa came running, her braid swinging from left to right. I bounced on my toes. The day was hot and dry. Dust swirled all around her. I'm going to try to write down the whole conversation again. I never want to forget it.

"Sorry," she said, her chest going up and down as she reached the window. "My mother wanted me to help her sweep and do the washing this morning." She focused on me. My hair hung lose and knotted around my face.

"Why don't you have your ribbon in?" she asked, grabbing hold of her woven hair, smoothing it.

"I want to wear it so much," I said. "But I'm afraid my papa will ask me about it."

Hafa cast her eyes down. "I understand."

"It's the best thing anyone ever gave me," I blurted out.

"It is? It's just a scrap of ribbon," she said, lighting back up.

"She didn't have any friends back home," Amil said.

At first I glared at Amil, but he was only telling the truth. Maybe it was hard for him to have friends, knowing I didn't. I guess he didn't count Sabeen. Maybe he always felt like he was abandoning me. I was so in my own thoughts I didn't hear any footsteps, just a small yelp from Amil. Then a hand clamped down on my shoulder. Hafa turned and ran before anyone said anything.

"Leave the window," Papa growled behind me. I stole a glance at Hafa before I moved away, her braid coming loose as she ran back to her house.

"Haven't we had enough trouble? Are you trying to get us killed?" Papa hissed at us, his eyes fierce. Normally he would have yelled, but he knew he couldn't here.

Amil and I backed up against the wall.

"She's not going to tell anyone," Amil said.

"You don't understand, do you?" Papa leaned in, his face an inch away from Amil's. A tiny speck of spit flew out of his mouth and landed on Amil's cheek. Amil didn't move.

"Please, Papa. Don't be mad at Amil. It was my fault. I just wanted a friend, someone else to talk to," I said.

Papa turned his angry gaze to me. "I doubt that. And if that truly was the case, then I've been wrong all along telling you to talk more. Maybe we're all better off when you keep your mouth shut," Papa said. His words sank in deep, stinging all the way. My throat tightened with shame.

He shook his head. "We'll have to go now." He walked out, leaving me and Amil standing there, our arms hanging down at our sides. Then Amil grabbed my hand and held it, and we stood there for a moment before sitting down on my bed. I could hear Papa talking to Dadi and Dadi letting out a moaning "No, no."

We sat there silently for a long time afraid to leave our room until Papa called us for dinner. Nobody spoke. Nobody looked at us. Did Rashid Uncle know? Only the sounds of chewing and the clinking of bowls were heard. I felt blank, empty. I still do. No more sadness, no more fear. Just emptiness.

Papa is probably right. Everyone is better off when I don't talk. I'm not going to, Mama, ever again. I will be like Rashid Uncle. When I really need to say something I will write my words down on a chalkboard so they can be erased.

Love, Nisha

———————◈———————

September 11, 1947

Dear Mama,

We left at dawn. Papa said we had no choice, and he didn't want to wake Rashid Uncle. It was stay here and risk our lives or get on the train and risk our lives, and we might as well try to cross the border. It was our only hope. Papa says Dadi isn't strong enough to walk the whole way.

Hafa and I will never become normal friends who braid each other's hair, talk every day, and tell each other our secrets. Rashid Uncle and I won't spend time together where I could learn real stories about you, not just make up my own imaginary ones. Now it's all dust behind us.

While Rashid Uncle slept, Papa and Dadi quietly gathered our stuff in a pile. Papa packed a sweet potato, a pepper, and two tomatoes in his bag, all the fresh food that Rashid Uncle had. He also took a stack of chapatis and a big bag of dry rice.

I'm losing a part of you all over again, Mama. It's like my heart is cracked in half and will never be whole again. Why did I need to talk to Hafa so badly? If we die on the train, that will be our fault, too. If we survive, will I ever live without this shame?

I rolled up my mat and net and picked up my bag. I thought about how I would never say a proper good-bye to Rashid Uncle after everything he had done for us. I thought of him having to be lonely again. I think he was starting to like having us around. Lately I had noticed him humming when he carved at night. Then I saw it, the half-carved doll on his stool, waiting to be finished. A newer, sharper sadness swept over me. I wondered if I should take it, but then he would never finish it. While Papa and Dadi moved around I quickly went to our room like I was looking for something and wrote these words fast and steady:

*Dear Rashid Uncle,*

*It's my fault we left. I only wanted a friend.
Did you ever want a friend so badly you didn't
care what happened to you? I hope we see you
again. Thank you for cooking with me. Thank
you for telling me about my mother. Don't
worry about the doll. I hope it's beautiful and
that you sell it for a lot of rupees. Please come
find us one day. Please forgive me.*

*Your niece, Nisha*

I never got a chance to leave the note for Uncle. Papa
found me and told me if I didn't stop writing in my silly
book, he'd take it away. I quickly stuffed it in my bag,
and he hurried us out. Maybe I will mail it someday.
We stood there outside for a moment, blinking in the
dawn. I don't know what I expected us to do, but it all
seemed too easy after hiding for so many days. On my
way out, I was surprised to see Papa wrote something
for Rashid Uncle on his chalkboard which lay on the
dining room table. I remember every word:

*Dearest Rashid,*

*We had to leave suddenly. The girl next door saw us, so be careful. I can never repay you for your kindness, and I hope we didn't put you in any danger. Faria has been watching. I feel her. Thank you.*

I sucked in my breath when I read your name. I always call you Mama, always think of you as Mama. I didn't realize that I forgot your name until I heard it. But then, to see your name like that, *Faria,* written by Papa. It felt like freezing water on my face. Faria, Faria, Faria. It reminds me of the whole person you were, beyond my mama. It gives me chills as I write it.

"Why didn't we say good-bye to Rashid Uncle?" Amil whispered after we were several feet away. I could hear tears in the back of his voice.

"The less involved he is, the better. If you both hadn't been so stupid, we would have. I'm trying to keep you safe, don't you see?" He ran his hands through his black thinning hair streaked with gray. I hadn't ever seen Papa so upset. I've seen him angrier, but this was different. His eyes were unfocused. His voice sounded higher.

Papa said the quicker we could get to the main path without being seen, the better. Then we would blend in more. The miles went by quickly, and we passed around the water, vegetables, and chapatis, never stopping to rest. As we came near the village, the crowds started to thicken. Papa's eyes widened in fear as we got closer to the crowd. He told us to hold hands and stay together.

Amil and I held hands tightly and Papa held on to both mine and Dadi's arm. We moved slowly as a linked foursome, pushing into the village by midday. There was a line for the train tickets a hundred people long. We got on it. There were mostly families in front of us, looking dirty and tired. Nobody spoke to one another. I thought about the market and festivals back home, how everyone talked to everyone, chatting about which pepper looked ripe, who was getting married, who had a baby, who was sick, who was moving. Anything and everything, words spilling out of mouths easily.

"There is a train every few hours," Papa said.

228 ❖ THE NIGHT DIARY

We nodded and stood and stood. The line moved slowly, then stopped. The ticket man yelled out that he was out of tickets and wouldn't sell more until after the train came. The sun beat down on us and we had small sips of water and shifted our weight from foot to foot. The family in front of us had a baby that the mother held in a sling on her side and two young boys. They stared at us until the father shook them and they turned around.

When the train came, I heard it before I saw it, the sound of metal grinding against metal, the squeal of the brakes. Everyone turned and some started to rush toward it. Many people left the line to try and get on. The train overflowed with people, people sticking their heads out the windows for air, men sitting on the roof and hanging off the sides. Papa lay a heavy hand on my shoulder.

"Stay back. We're going to have to wait for the next one."

There were angry people waving tickets. Some climbed onto the steps, forcing themselves on. Some younger men climbed on top. The conductor got out and tried to push people away, but there were too many and he couldn't stop them. We stood back and watched. The man in front of us started yelling to his family. "The next one will be packed, too. Tickets don't matter at a time like this!"

Then he turned to us. "Save yourselves and get on that train. Who knows when the next one will come."

"It's too crowded, too dangerous," Papa said.

I wondered if we couldn't get on the next one, would we sneak back into Rashid Uncle's house. I hoped we would.

The man ran forward with his wife, the baby, and the two boys. One of the boys fell and the crowds moved over him toward the train. Suddenly I couldn't see him anymore and the rest of the family didn't notice. The man found an entrance and ran up to the stairs and waved his family over. He climbed up, pulling one son in with him. The wife then noticed the other boy was missing. She yelled out, turning wildly around in circles looking for him. Other people forced themselves in front of her and the man and boy disappeared inside. The train started to move now. She ran with her baby alongside it, but the other boy had gotten up and found her. He called to her, waving. She stopped and grabbed him and held him to her as they watched the train leave, the man and the other brother gone.

I wanted to tell Papa so badly. I tugged on Papa's sleeve.

"What?" he barked at me, his eyes flashing.

I pointed to the woman who was still near the tracks about thirty feet away crouched down on the ground, crying with her baby and her son. I could see through the spaces between crowds that the boy had his arm around her trying to comfort her. But Papa didn't see.

"What?" he said again.

"What is it?" Amil said. I couldn't speak, not even to Amil. It was like my brain had shut that part of me down completely. I searched for my diary and pencil to write him a note. There were so many people rushing around now, yelling and pushing, but we stayed in the line. How could Papa not have not noticed the family? How was I going to explain it all? I swallowed. Another family went over to comfort her—a father, mother, two older girls, and two younger boys.

I pointed again.

"Nisha," Papa said impatiently, looking out at the sea of bodies all around us. "Please tell me what you're pointing at."

It looked like the woman was being helped by the other family. They were talking to her, helping her up. I guess there was nothing Papa could do.

I just shook my head and stared back down at my feet. What if there wasn't anyone to help her and I couldn't explain? I was a useless girl. I should let them all get on the train without me. Then they wouldn't have to worry about another body, my useless body, to fill with water and food anymore.

We finally got tickets and a few hours later, another train came. By this time, we had moved forward and stood near the tracks.

Papa circled us with his arms, holding us close together. "Don't wait for anyone to get off! Just get on!" he yelled over the noise.

I held my breath. I wasn't brave enough to run away. Papa, Amil, they would only look for me and we'd never escape. Then I would be even more useless.

Maybe if we get to a new home, I could slip quietly out the door one morning. They would search for me, but would soon realize it was easier without me. I am just a small, silent drop of nothing who attracts angry men and wants to be friends with the wrong girl and can't even make herself speak in order to save a mother and her children.

The train stopped. Papa eyed it quickly. It looked as crowded as the other train, but it was too late now. I saw the mother, sitting again, rocking her baby, huddling her other boy to her. No one was around them. What was going to happen to them?

"Go," Papa said, and shoved us toward the opening doors. I held Amil's hand tight, Dadi holding my other arm, Papa behind us pushing. We spilled up the stairs and flooded into the car. All the seats were filled. The corners were filled. We moved into the aisle.

The hot, soggy air hit my nose, and I scrunched my eyes closed at the sting of the horrible smell. I glanced around me as we jostled into the middle. Everyone looked dirty, hungry, and scared. Some of these people had probably been on the train for more than a day. I could hear yelling and crying from the people outside who couldn't get on. The conductors were trying to block the train and then it started moving. Good-bye, Kazi; good-bye, Rashid Uncle; and your house, Mama; good-bye, Hafa; good-bye, old India.

Love, Nisha

September 12, 1947

I have seen things I never thought I'd see. There were men fighting. There was blood. I don't know if the train will stop and more fighting will happen and more people will be killed, including us. If anyone finds this, please send it to Kazi Syed in Mirpur Khas. Please remember us. Please remember the way it used to be when India was whole.

———————◈———————

September 26, 1947

Dear Mama,

It has been two weeks since I last wrote. At first I couldn't write and tell you what happened, but now I must. Maybe if I put it in here, you can help me carry it. When I last wrote we were on the train. We had traveled for about an hour or so and then the train started to slow down. I couldn't see out the window because I was sitting on the floor, but I saw lots of people looking out.

"Why are we slowing down?" Dadi asked.

"They're stopping the train!" a man called out.

Papa grabbed us by our arms and made us stand up. Then he pushed through all the people and looked out, too.

I noticed Dadi's hands, the soft blue-gray of her veins resting under her thin, dry brown skin. I follow her veins to the tips of her fingers. They shook. That's what I remember before everything changed—her fingers shaking like a picture on a wall just as an earthquake happens. Mama, I can't tell you yet. I thought I could but it's making me feel sick. I'll try again tomorrow.

Love, Nisha

September 27, 1947

Dear Mama,

This time I will tell you as best I can, I promise. I don't remember all of it. There are places where my memory goes blank. Maybe I even saw more. But I will tell you what I remember.

There were men, probably about four of them. They must have blocked the tracks. I just know the train slowed and the brakes screeched and we were all thrown forward on top of one another. There were bodies tumbling, feet in people's faces. Amil and Dadi fell on top of me in a heap. After a few moments we righted ourselves.

I heard the yelling before I saw them. I watched Dadi's hands shake, and I heard the sounds getting louder and louder. The sounds of angry feet hitting the ground, denting the earth. The women in our car held their children close. Dadi, Amil, and I huddled together as low as we could, and Papa watched out the window.

"Get back," Papa suddenly yelled, moving us away from the main door, pressing us toward the middle.

Two conductors pushed passed us, not yelling but screaming, waving knives. One had a gun. Have you ever heard a grown man scream, Mama? It's so strange. Everything felt like it was happening in slow motion and that I wasn't in my body, like the way I felt when the man pressed the knife against my throat. I hoped it was a dream and I had fallen asleep on the floor of the train.

The men had climbed up the stairs, had started to enter our car, but our conductors managed to force them back down the stairs. They all waved their weapons, making high-pitched and deafening sounds, beyond human. I covered my ears. One conductor stepped on my bare toe, crushed it, as he trampled past. I looked down and saw blood by the nail. I watched it run down my toe until Amil pulled me toward him and Dadi.

Papa stood in front guarding us, his hands out. Dadi, Amil, and I crouched with other women and children. There was a mother right next to us, clutching her three children, a baby and two young girls. I could feel one of the girl's breath on my cheek. It smelled sour. The women murmured prayers. Amil and I squeezed each other's hands and this is what I thought: If I die, I'm glad I'm here with my brother, the other half of me.

They fought outside. At that point, Papa and many other passengers rushed to the window to see. Amil pulled me to a bottom crack of one of the windows and we watched, our heads pressed against strangers' heads. The men punched and sliced at each other. A man yelled out that the Hindus were murderers. The men from our train accused Muslims of the same. Some of the passengers started to respond to the accusations and rush out to join the other men, their wives pulling on their arms begging them not to go. There was blood. A lot of blood. A man's leg slashed, a man's throat slashed. A man stabbed in the chest. Then a gun shot. There were Sikh men, too, everyone trying to kill one another. A Muslim man fell. A Hindu man fell. A Sikh man fell, his turban unraveling. I saw a Muslim man lying on the ground, his throat slashed, his eyes rolled back. He had fallen right next to a Hindu conductor whose chest was bleeding heavily. They lay close together, hands touching. They would die like that. And I watched them, Mama. I watched them die like that.

The train started to move. The Hindu men who were still alive jumped back on. I looked at the dying men on the ground. For what? I did not know. More revenge? I shook all over. I had never seen anyone kill before. It has changed me. I used to think people were mostly good, but now I wonder if anyone could be a murderer. Who was the first one, Mama, the first to kill when they decided to break apart India?

Shortly after we rolled away, my head felt light and everything went dark. I don't remember anything else until Papa shook me. Amil and Dadi were huddled next to me. Had I fainted? Had I fallen asleep on the floor of the train? How much time had passed?

Papa shook my shoulder gently, his eyes glassy. "Amil, Nisha, we're here," he said.

Love, Nisha

September 28, 1947

Dear Mama,

I didn't even tell you where we are now. We're in Jodhpur. We're in the new India. The old one is all gone. We are staying in a one-room flat over a spice shop that Raj Uncle and Rupesh Uncle arranged for us. It has a small kitchen area with a sink and a stove. Cracked green and yellow tiles cover the floor. There is a washroom with a drain in the floor, and a chain attached to the shower spout that dumps blasts of cold water on you, and a toilet room at the end of the hallway outside our flat. The water only runs a few hours a day, but at least there is running water. When we first arrived, there were sand and ants everywhere, but we cleaned it up as best we could. Still, it's not easy to live in one dark, dusty room. I don't know how long we will be here.

Somehow when we were walking, I couldn't imagine being alone, would never want to. But now that we're out of danger I miss sitting in the garden at our old house on the hill watching the sunset or being alone in the bedroom when Amil wasn't there, or secretly poking around Papa's room or the kitchen. There was always something to explore, always a place to be alone and quiet. I also miss Rashid Uncle's house, your house. I miss lying on the couch reading books even if we couldn't go outside.

Now there's a wooden table and chairs and a space for all our bedrolls, that's it. Nothing is on the sandstone walls. We have a roof. We are alive. We are safe. So how can I complain? How do I dare complain when so many others didn't make it here? Raj Uncle and Rupesh Uncle and their families live down the block in similar flats, and we all have dinner together at our place or their places, my five cousins, Amil, and I sitting on the floor around a mat with dented metal plates in our laps. It's good to see them here, but I can only think of everything we lost. Does that mean I'm a terrible person?

I think a lot about our mango trees, so many of them. I think about the sound of insects and birds at dusk. I think about the sugarcane, and Kazi. I think about Kazi all the time. I want to pretend I don't miss him, but I do a lot. In some ways, he was my only real friend.

Jodhpur is a big, hot city. The only thing I like about it is that nobody is trying to kill us here and that many of the houses are painted a beautiful blue.

Will my bad dreams ever stop? Will I ever not think about the things I saw on the train? It runs through my head every day, like a radio on in the background. Papa told us after we got here, after we settled down and were safe, that thousands of people have died crossing the border both ways. Maybe the gods were watching over us, he said, and Papa never talks like that. He also said that it wasn't even so dangerous where we were. He said that all kinds of people—men, women, and children—have been killed in unthinkable ways and are still being killed. He said that trains pulled up to stops filled with dead people from both sides of the border. Everyone blames one another. Hindus, Muslims, Sikhs, they have all done awful things. But what have I done? What has Papa, or Dadi, or Amil done? What has Kazi done? I want to know who I can blame, Mama, for the nightmares that wake me up every night now. It must be someone's fault. Maybe I'll blame everyone.

Love, Nisha

October 3, 1947

Dear Mama,

We have been here now almost three weeks. I haven't been writing. I don't know why. My brain is filled with sludge. I feel so sad all the time. Aren't I supposed to be happy now?

Amil and I started school last week. I'm learning Hindi now, which helps keep my mind off the things I don't want to think about. I never speak it out loud, though. Papa found a clinic to work in. Dadi sweeps the flat over and over and sings again and writes letters that she won't let anyone see. I still don't talk to anyone, not even to Amil, and he has stopped asking. He will make friends now at school and won't care so much. I feel terrible that I've even shut out Amil, but I just can't make myself speak. It's not a choice. The words just won't come out. When I imagine my words out loud, they seem so deafening, as if the sound could actually hurt someone. At least things are better with Papa and Amil. Ever since we came here, Papa is kinder to him and tries to help him with his schoolwork. I think it's because Papa really had to imagine

Amil being gone forever, and he saw how terrible that would be.

Papa also keeps begging me to talk. Papa has never done that. He knelt down before me last night with tears in his eyes and told me he was sorry if he treated me too harshly when we left Rashid Uncle's, that none of it mattered now, that the important thing was that we were safe and alive. He asked me to forgive him. He asked me what he could do. I've never seen him like this. What can I tell him? That it's better for everyone if I don't talk? That the only words I have left to say are the ones no one wants to hear and even if I wanted to, my body won't let me? Instead I pat his shoulder. *I'm okay, Papa,* I write on a scrap of paper and show it to him. He reads it and tells me I don't have to be so brave anymore. I am so stunned, I drop my pencil. Papa thinks I'm brave? Why on earth would he think that?

After school everyday, I go to the market with Amil and Dadi and we buy our food. I do all the cooking now. Papa and Dadi let me. I even cook for Raj Uncle's and Rupesh Uncle's families. Nobody cares anymore if I grow up to be a cook. I should be happy about that, but it's not a happy or sad feeling. It's just something I must do. The smell of the rice boiling, the feel of my knife cutting through a fresh tomato, the sizzle of onions and mustard seed hitting the pan. It's the only thing that makes me feel better.

Last night Raj Uncle brought a radio with him and we listened to it while we ate dinner. It was Gandhiji's birthday. The radio announcer said Gandhi spent his birthday fasting and spinning yarn on his wheel. He also said that many people came to visit the Mahatma and offer him good wishes, but Gandhi wasn't joyous. He was heartbroken because Hindus and Muslims were still fighting and killing one another. I understand how he feels. When Gandhiji spins, maybe he finds some peace like I do when I cook.

Love, Nisha

❖

October 5, 1947

Dear Mama,

There is a girl at school. She's very small and wears her hair in two braids, one on either side. She follows me around, but doesn't say anything, and of course I don't say anything to her. She sits next to me in the classroom and sits next to me at lunch and we both don't talk to anyone. Sometimes she looks at me and smiles a little bit, but it makes me scared to look her in the eye, so I quickly look down. I don't even know her name. I wonder if she's from Jodhpur or if she came here like me. Did she see anyone die? Did she see worse things than I did? I want to ask her these questions, but I can't. I am broken. I am broken on top of broken.

The school is a lot bigger than the one I used to go to. It's also mixed, boys and girls. I'm glad to be back in school. I like to put my head down and write my words, do my sums, and try not to think about anything else. I keep my pencils very sharp. But then there's this girl. I wish she'd leave me alone.

Love, Nisha

October 15, 1947

Dear Mama,

Something has happened. I still don't think it's real which is why I haven't told you. I think I have to wait to write about it because I'm afraid I'm dreaming. If I write about it, I might wake up. I think it's a gift from you, Mama. How else could something like this happen?

Love, Nisha

October 18, 1947

Dear Mama,

It's been three days and I'm ready to write it down because now I believe it's real. When Amil and I came home from school, there was a man squatting in our alley on the way to the back stairs that take us up to our little flat. He crouched, skinny and filthy, his hair and beard overgrown and matted. Amil took my arm.

"Let's go get Papa at the clinic," he said quietly, pulling me away.

I nodded, but was thinking of Dadi inside. What if she came out to go to the market? He looked too weak to be dangerous. The man started to reach his hand out. Amil and I backed away.

"Amil, Nisha," the man croaked. How did he know our names? He looked at us, his bony face tilting up, his eyes connecting with mine. I knew those eyes. I knew that voice. It felt like I had been riding on the crest of a high wave and now it tumbled onto shore.

"Kazi," I whispered, and sank to my knees. It wasn't hard to say his name. It was like my voice had been waiting for this moment.

Amil ran to him and helped him up. He put his arms around him. I was crying, trembling, my face in my hands. I was afraid to look up, afraid I had just imagined it was him, and that it was just someone looking for food.

"Nisha," Amil called out. "Help me."

I raised my head slowly and saw that it was still Kazi. His face contorted like he was crying, but no tears came. I walked over and gently took his hand which was caked with dirt. Through my blurred eyes, I pinched the skin lightly on the back of his hand like Papa did to me when we had no water. His skin stayed in a little bunch.

"He needs a doctor. Go," I said to Amil. "Go get Papa."

It was strange that I was the one with words suddenly. Amil stared at me for a second.

"Go," I told him, and gave him a light push on his chest. "I will bring him upstairs," I said.

"Are you sure?" Amil asked.

"Yes, please go fast."

Amil touched Kazi's arm and ran off.

"How did you—" I started to say, but Kazi stopped me.

"Later," he managed to say.

I had spoken enough for someone to stop me, for Kazi to stop me. If he didn't look so weak and sick, I would have jumped up and down for joy. This couldn't be real, I thought. Maybe we had died on the train and we were reincarnated and living a different life now. He put his arm around me. His sharp, sweaty smell was familiar. It smelled like the walk we took to get here. It smelled like pain. We struggled up the stairs to see Dadi.

"Oh!" Dadi exclaimed, and put her hand to her mouth as we came in.

"It's Kazi, it's Kazi," I said, not believing my words.

Dadi nodded and cried a little and helped him over to a chair. He slumped in it. I knelt before him as Dadi got some water and a bowl of rice.

I held the cup to his lips. He sipped slowly. I fed him small bites of rice, then bigger.

"Go slow," Dadi said, her tears still spilling out, patting his hand over and over.

Kazi's here, with us.

When Papa came back, my voice retreated. He checked Kazi from head to toe, listened to his heartbeat, measured his blood pressure. Kazi ate and drank a little more, and Papa took Kazi into the washroom to help him clean up. Then Papa got Kazi set up on his bedroll. We all knelt around him.

"I had to come and find you. You are my family. I don't have my own, you know. I have no siblings. My parents are dead. Dadi wrote me and told me where you were," he said before he fell into a deep sleep.

"It's a miracle," she said as she cried softly and held his hand.

That night, Papa slept on a thin blanket on the floor

with only a shirt rolled up as a pillow. Amil and I both offered Papa our pillows. But he turned them down.

"Is Kazi going to be okay?" Amil whispered before we all fell asleep.

"I think so," Papa said, shaking his head.

"Is Kazi allowed to stay with us, you know because he's—" Amil started to ask.

"He's family," Papa only said.

As I went to sleep that night, I felt peaceful in a way I never had before. We were put back together. To Nehru, Jinnah, India, and Pakistan, to the men who fight and kill—you can't split us. You can't split love.

Sometimes I think about why we get to be alive when so many others died for no reason walking the same walk, crossing the same border. All that suffering, all that death, for nothing. I will never understand, as long as I live, how a country could change overnight from only a line drawn.

But at least I didn't have to wonder anymore what would happen to Kazi or if he would live with another family. That feeling is so new, like a brilliant jewel I can't stop staring at. At least this hole in my heart is filled. I can cook with him again. I can talk with him. For some reason he is the only person I want to talk to.

Love, Nisha

---

November 10, 1947

Dear Mama,

There is something else I haven't told you yet. Kazi brought a piece of one of your paintings, just a folded square of canvas ripped from its frame, the paint chipped. It's the hand holding the egg. I almost fainted when he showed it to us. How did he know how special it was to me? My mind went swirling back to our home, back to the place where Papa kept your paintings. Here was a piece of you, brought to us from the ashes of our old life. Papa walked forward and took it.

"Thank you," he said, his hand on Kazi's shoulder. It looked liked tears had formed in Papa's eyes, but he blinked and they were gone. That was a few weeks ago. Yesterday, Papa came home and hung a picture on the wall. He had gotten the piece of your painting reframed. It's much smaller than it was, but the important part is there. The hand. The egg. He hung it on the wall over our table.

Kazi is cooking again, and I'm not just his helper. We cook together, Kazi and I, in this little kitchen. He went to the market with Amil as soon as he felt well enough and brought back ingredients for sai bhaji, the dish that will always remind me of home. We lined up the spinach, tomatoes, onions, chilies, and other ingredients on the table. Then I got the mortar and pestle I had been keeping in my bag by my bedroll. I hadn't wanted to look at it since we got here. It was too sad. I had been wrapping our spices in a thin towel and crushing them with a rock.

I brought it to him and held it out. Kazi smiled wide at me and nodded.

"Good girl," he said. "It's yours now."

I washed it out and put a handful of cumin seeds in the bowl. I pressed them down with the pestle, the white marble cool and heavy in my hand. I've never thought I could feel so happy crushing spices.

Papa is trying to find us a bigger flat so we can have more rooms and furniture, but I kind of like it here now. This will always be the place where we started to live again. This is where Kazi came back and made me feel loved. He risked his life to be with us. Would I have done the same?

Still, it will be good to have more space and real beds. I think about our old compound, the main room, the hallways, our bedroom, Papa's room, the study, the gardens, Kazi's own cottage. I didn't know we were so rich until we became poor. But Papa is working hard at the clinic and I don't think we will be poor forever. Jodhpur is okay, very hot, but the people are friendly. Nobody asks about Kazi. They just go about their business. Kazi doesn't wear his topi outside anymore. I wonder if that bothers him. He shares Papa's clothes. He still does his prayers on a little mat that Papa found for him. When I hear his low chanting words, it fills me up. Sometimes I hear Dadi's high-pitched singing in the background, her Hindu songs and Kazi's Muslim prayers, a sweet, rich music together.

I'm sorry I'm writing less. It could be because life has become more normal, but I'm so happy I made this space for you—this space for us. It's where I can go to find you whenever I need to. I will always tell you the important things and I promise, Mama, no matter what happens, you will never be alone.

Remember that girl at school? She finally talked to me. She asked me my name, but I couldn't answer her. I just looked down at my lap. Then she did something amazing. She leaned in. She put her hand on my shoulder. She told me it was okay, and she told me I didn't have to talk. I felt tears swelling in my eyes. I wrote her *thank you* on my notepad and held it up. Then I wrote, *my name is Nisha*. She told me her name was Sumita. No girl at school has ever been so kind to me.

I have decided something. I will try to speak to Sumita, if it's the last thing I do. I want you to see me have a real friend, and I want to feel the way I felt with Hafa. It may take me a long time, but I will try because Sumita is the first person who ever told me that it's okay to just be myself. I want to be brave, but Mama, maybe I already am.

Love, Nisha

# *Author's Note*

During the days of August 14 and August 15, 1947, India gained independence from British rule and was partitioned into two republics, India and Pakistan. The partition came after centuries of religious tension between Indian Hindus and Indian Muslims. There were many people who did not want India split into two countries, but it was ultimately agreed upon by the leaders in charge.

In certain places across India, conflicts would break out periodically. However, before partition there were areas where people of many religions, including Muslims, Hindus, Sikhs, and smaller religious populations such as Parsis, Christians, and Jains, lived side by side harmoniously. During the crossing of borders, tensions greatly increased and fighting and killing took place between Muslims entering Pakistan and Hindus and people of other religions entering India. Much of the violence happened in places where it had been peaceful before. It is estimated that over 14 million people crossed the borders and at least one million people died during this exchange (some say more, some say less). It is the largest mass migration in history.

The fictional family depicted in this novel lived in one such area, and their experiences are loosely based on my father's side of the family. My father, with his parents and siblings (my grandparents, aunts, and uncles), had to travel across the border from Mirpur Khas to Jodhpur just like the main character, Nisha, does in this book. My father's family made the journey safely, but lost their home, many belongings, and had to start over in an unfamiliar place as refugees. I wanted to understand more about what my relatives went through which is a big reason why I wrote this book.

The major figures in power during this time were Mohammed Ali Jinnah, leader of the Muslim League; Jawaharlal Nehru, leader of the Indian National Congress; Lord Mountbatten, the British Viceroy who was sent to India to lead the transition toward independence; and Mahatma Gandhi, the former leader of the Indian National Congress and a nonviolent antiwar activist. Jinnah felt that the Muslim minority would not be fairly represented in the new Indian government and wanted a separate state. Nehru and Gandhi did not want to see India split and believed that a united India would be a better India. All those in power wanted peaceful relations between the groups, but disagreed on the best way to make that happen.

There have been and continue to be many theories about who played a bigger role in creating this conflict. Many blame the "other side" for the violence that ensued, and many people who suffered horrible acts and lost family members can never feel forgiveness for their attackers. Nisha and her family's journey was harder than some, including my father's, and easier than others. This story is a combination of known history and imagined scenarios to create one possible story that could have taken place at this time.

Tensions still exist between certain groups of Hindus and Muslims today, as well as between many religious groups all over the world. Remembering the mistakes of the past will hopefully create a more enlightened, tolerant, and peaceful future. Accepting differences has always been a great challenge for humanity played out in thousands of ways. This was one way.

# *Glossary*

ALOO TIKKI: A fried potato patty made with onions and spices.

BANSURI: A side-blown bamboo flute often played in Indian
classical music.

BINDI: A dot Hindu women sometimes wear in the center of
their forehead to signify different things regarding religion,
class, and marital status.

CHAPATI: A small, flat unleavened pan-cooked bread.

CRICKET: A very popular game using a bat and ball played in
India, Pakistan, England, Australia, and around the world.

DADI: A Hindi, Sindhi, and Urdu word meaning one's grand-mother on the paternal side.

DAL: A simple stew made of split lentils or split peas and spices. It can also mean dried split lentils or split peas.

DHOTI: A male garment which consists of a piece of fabric wrapped around the waist that covers the legs.

DIWALI: A joyous and popular Hindu holiday. It is a festival of light that takes place over five days. Houses are cleaned and decorated in preparation. People dress in new clothes and offer prayers to one or more deities. They also gather with friends and family for candle lighting, fireworks, gift giving, and food. The holiday signifies the triumph of light over darkness.

DUPATTA: A scarf typically worn with an outfit called a salwar kameez.

GHEE: Butter that is clarified, or has the milk solids and water removed during cooking.

GULAB JAMUN: A dessert made from deep fried milk powder balls coated in rosewater syrup.

HINDU: A follower of Hinduism, the world's oldest known organized religion still being practiced today. Hinduism is a religion with a diverse philosophy based on several deity figures and texts—the Vedas, the Upanishads, the Mahabharata, and the Ramayana. There are over one billion Hindus living in the world today, with the majority of Hindus living in India.

JI: A suffix added to names as a term of honor and respect, as in Gandhiji.

JODHPUR: A medium-size city in the Indian state of Rajasthan.

KAJU KATLI: A diamond-shaped candy made from sweetened pressed cashews.

KEBAB: A dish consisting of sliced or ground meat with spices, often grilled on a skewer. Vegetables or cheese can be used as well.

KHEER: A sweet pudding usually made with rice and milk, flavored with cardamom, saffron, raisins, or nuts.

KURTA: A long tunic-style shirt.

LORD BRAHMA, VISHNU, AND SHIVA: Three Hindu deities that Hindus believe are responsible for the creation, preservation, and destruction of the universe. Lord Brahma is the creator of the universe. Vishnu is the preserver. Shiva is the destroyer so Lord Brahma can create again.

(THE) MAHABHARATA: An ancient Indian epic poem as well as the longest-known epic poem ever written. It is a major text in Hinduism. It follows the fate of two warring groups of cousins, the Kauravas and the Pandavas.

MIRPUR KHAS: A medium-size city in the Sindh province of Pakistan.

MUSLIM: A follower of the religion Islam. Islam began in the seventh century by the prophet Muhammad. Muslims follow the teachings of a text called the Quran. There are approximately 1.6 billion Muslims living in the world today with the majority of Muslims living in the Middle East, North Africa, Central Asia, and South Asia.

MUTTON BIRYANI: A rice dish made with basmati rice, mutton (goat meat or meat from a mature sheep), herbs, and spices.

PAKORA: A snack usually consisting of a piece of vegetable like potato, cauliflower, or pepper deep fried in a seasoned batter.

PARATHA: A layered flatbread, most often stuffed with potatoes, onions, or spinach.

POORI: An unleavened deep-fried bread that puffs up when fried.

PUJA: An act of Hindu prayer which usually includes providing an offering to the divine such as food, flowers, or lighting a candle.

PUNJAB: A province in British-ruled India before Partition. After Partition, Punjab was split into two parts, with the western section belonging to Pakistan and the eastern section belonging to India. It was an area of extreme rioting and horrific violence during Partition.

RASMALAI: A dessert made from soft cheese patties in a sweet, creamy sauce.

ROTI: A general term for flatbread cooked in a pan or oven and is interchangeable with chapati.

RUPEE: The basic unit of money in India and Pakistan.

SAI BHAJI: A spinach curry common to the area of Sindh, Pakistan, where the city of Mirpur Khas is located.

SALWAR KAMEEZ: A female garment that can be simple or fancy. The salwar are pants gathered at the bottom and the kameez is a long tunic shirt.

SAMOSA: A small triangular-shaped fried pastry filled with spiced vegetables or meat.

Sari: A garment worn by women made of decorative fabric that is wrapped in a special way around the body.

Sikh: A follower of Sikhism, which originated in the Punjab region of India in the fifteenth century based on the teachings of Guru Nanak. The majority of Sikhs live in Punjab, India, but reside all over the world. There are over twenty-six million Sikhs in the world today.

Sitar: A fretted string instrument most often played in Indian classical music.

Tabla: A pair of hand drums where one drum is larger than the other. It is commonly used in Indian classical music.

Topi: A circular prayer cap worn by Muslim men in India and Pakistan.

Umerkot: A town in the Sindh province of Pakistan.

# *Acknowledgments*

It takes a lot of people to publish one book and therefore I'm grateful to many:

I don't know what I'd do without my agent, Sara Crowe at Pippin Properties. She's one of the best in the business, who not only magically keeps selling my work, but has been a pleasure getting to know over the years.

I also don't know how I got so lucky to be able to work with editor extraordinaire, Namrata Tripathi, whose brilliant and gentle editorial guidance and perspective got this story where it needed to be. A true gift.

A huge thanks to everyone at Kokila and Dial, including Lauri Hornik, Stacey Friedberg, and Sydnee Monday; copy editor Rosanne Lauer; managing editors Kristen Tozzo and Natalie Vielkind; and everyone in production working on the book; the design team, Kristin Smith, Kelley Brady, Jenny Kelly, and Jasmin Rubero; the marketing team, including Emily Romero, Erin Berger, and Rachel Cone-Gorham; the publicity team headed up by Shanta Newlin; the School and Library marketing team, including Carmela Iaria and Venessa Carson; the sales team led by Debra Polansky; and everyone in the warehouse, packing and shipping these books!

To my gem of a writing group, the extremely talented Sheela Chari, Sayantani Das Gupta, and Heather Tomlinson, who have been cheering me on since the very first word.

To my dear friends Sarah and Adel Hinawi whose valuable perspective helped me shape this novel.

To my generous and loving mother, Anita Hiranandani, who always makes me feel like I can do anything I've ever wanted to do even when I don't.

To my sister, Shana Hiranandani, who's able to bring me back from the edge when life and writing spills over. Thanks also to her wife, Netania Shapiro, for being a trusted reader and friend.

To my in-laws Phyllis and Hank Beinstein who

have tirelessly supported my family and my writing over many years.

To my husband, David Beinstein, a talented writer and forever loving supporter, whose willingness to read draft after draft and man the ship when I'm on a deadline never goes away, even when I don't shower. Also to my beautiful children, Hannah and Eli, who inspire me to work hard because I see them work so hard every single day.

Last, but so not least, I must thank my father, Hiro Hiranandani, whose personal experiences inspired me to write about Partition and whose love, resilience, and rock solid presence in my life has given me so much. Thanks also to his willingness to share his stories and have many conversations, random e-mails, and spontaneous texts about the accuracy of Nisha's world. It was truly the backbone of this book. I also want to acknowledge my father's parents, my grandparents, Rewachand and Motilbai; his sisters, my aunts, Padma and Drupadi; and his brothers, my uncles, Naru, Gul, Vishnu, and Lachman; and the millions of lives which were painfully altered forever from the Partition of India in 1947.

The best part about books is that they stay with you even after you finish them—you smell the food that the characters made, see the sights described on the page, and think about the world from the perspective of someone other than yourself. Turn the page for questions that might help you discuss *The Night Diary* with friends, family, or classmates. Afterward, and with adult supervision, try the author's family recipe for Sai Bhaji, one of Nisha's favorite dishes.

# Discussion Questions

1.  Why is it easier for Nisha to share her thoughts and feelings through a diary than through talking? Do you identify with this? How or how not?

1b. How does Nisha express herself? What moments and people empower Nisha to make her voice heard? When does she feel frozen or unable to speak? In what ways does she grow?

2.  What motivates Nisha to write to her mama? Choose one of the following pages and dig into the reasons: 3, 8, 12, 13, 22, 40, 59, 63, 77, 97. How might Mama respond to Nisha?

3.  How are Amil and Nisha alike and different? What is the author trying to teach us through Amil's and Nisha's differences? In what ways do they have a special bond?

4. Food and cooking play a critical role in this story. How does food bring people together? Why is cooking so meaningful to Nisha? What activity brings you joy and peace like cooking brings her?

5. What significant moments occur at the good-bye party? (p.78)

6. Describe the relationship that Nisha and Amil have with Papa and how he reacts to each of them before, during, and after their journey.

7. Why is it difficult for Nisha to make friends? Why was she able to connect with Hafa so easily? How does the dramatic ending to that friendship impact Nisha?

8. Nisha writes, "I still don't understand. We were all part of the same country last month, all these different people and religions living together. Now we are supposed to separate and hate one another. Does Papa secretly hate Rashid Uncle? Does Rashid Uncle secretly hate us? Where do Amil and I fit in to all of this hate? Can you hate half of a person?" (pp.186–187) How is it confusing for Nisha to make sense of the news she hears around her?

9. A Muslim family saves Amil's life by accepting the family into shelter and providing them with space. (pp. 148–150) How does this scene celebrate humanity in a time of conflict?

10. When a man grabs Nisha and holds a knife to her throat, Papa lets the man go and says Gandhi's words, "An eye for an eye makes the whole world blind." (p. 171) Do you agree with the way that Papa responds?

11. Nisha has experiences that require her to grapple with concepts of fairness and social justice. Think about these issues by considering the following two quotations:

When Nisha thinks about the risks of talking with Hafa, she feels "a growing rage" in her chest and says, "It was okay for a strange man to put a knife at my throat, but it wasn't okay for us to speak to a little girl playing in the back of her house?" (p. 200)

Papa comes to the aid of a man at the water pump who "might have bled to death" (p. 136) without Papa's help. When Papa asks the man for a sip of his water, the man says, "Not enough" (p. 136) and he and his family leave.

Should Nisha talk to Hafa? Should the man give water to Papa? Why or why not?

12. How is the concept of splitting things in half and trying to make them whole explored in the book? How does it relate to Nisha's identity, to her nation, and to her personal story, which she says would "always have a line drawn through it, the before and the after."

13. *The Night Diary*, while historical fiction, can be thought of as a refugee story. Compare and contrast how Nisha's story is similar to that of present-day child refugees.

14. In what ways is Nisha's story one of hope and how does it celebrate diversity and humanity?

# Hiranandani family recipe for
# Sindhi Sai Bhaji

This recipe was passed down to me from my aunts. Sai Bhaji actually means green vegetables, so if you don't like spinach, you can substitute other greens. It's common to the area of Sindh, Pakistan, where my father was born.

1 box   zen chopped spinach (10 oz.) thawed

1 oni   opped

1 bu    fresh dill, washed and chopped

1-in   ube of ginger root, peeled and grated

5 cloves of garlic, peeled and minced

5 green chilies, chopped
(Serrano peppers are good. Use less if you want less heat.)

3 large tablespoons of rinsed chana dal
(dried yellow split chickpeas)

2 chopped tomatoes or ¼ cup of tomato sauce

1 teaspoon turmeric

1 teaspoon salt

2 cups of water

1 tablespoon vegetable oil

¼ cup of fresh lemon juice

Sauté onion, garlic, ginger, turmeric, and green chilies in pot with oil until softened. Then add the rest of the ingredients except for the lemon juice. Cook on low to medium heat until channa dal is soft, about 45 minutes. Then add lemon juice and cook for ten more minutes. After cooking, mash with a potato masher to blend ingredients. Salt to taste and serve warm as a side dish. Enjoy!

of fro
on, ch
nch of
ch c

**Veera Hiranandani** is the author of
*The Whole Story of Half a Girl*, which was
named a Sydney Taylor Notable Book and
a South Asian Book Award Finalist. She
teaches creative writing at Sarah Lawrence
College's Writing Institute.

Learn more at
veerahiranandani.com

or follow Veera
@veerahira.